SAVAGE SURRENDER

LEONA WHITE

Copyright © 2025 by Leona White

All rights reserved.

No part of this book may be reproduced in any form or by any electronic or mechanical means, including information storage and retrieval systems, without written permission from the author, except for the use of brief quotations in a book review.

❦ Created with Vellum

ALSO BY LEONA WHITE

Mafia Bosses Series

The Irish Arrangement || The Last Vendetta

The Constella Family

Under His Protection || Under His Watch || Under His Control || Under His Embrace

The Baranov Legacy

Guarded Rebellion || Savage Surrender

Holiday Mafia Standalone's

LEONA WHITE

Velvet Deception || Twin Deception

BLURB

I'm a man who deals in flesh and secrets.

Power flows through my veins like ice.

In my world of shadows, she walks into my classroom—*forbidden, untouchable.*

A Petrov princess with eyes that challenge and lips that beg for punishment.

She's half my age and twice as dangerous as any weapon I've wielded.

My mission was to spy on her, break her, make her family fall.

Instead, she's become my obsession, my weakness, **my savage addiction.**

But in our world of blood and betrayal, loving her could start a war.

She doesn't know I'm the enemy, that I belong to the family she's sworn to destroy.

And by the time she learns the truth, it'll be too late—I'm never letting her go.

Author's Note: A dangerous cocktail of forbidden desire: mafia wars meet professor-student romance. Features age gap, virgin heroine, and deliciously dark punishment scenes. For mature readers only.

1

VIKTOR

Travelers pushed and shoved. Every which way in the airport, they grumbled and complained, wheeling luggage and carrying bags that seemed stuffed too full for their comfort. Sweaty, red faces showed everywhere in the sea of people crowding New York's busiest airport, evidence of all the anger from dealing with flight delays and the exertion of wearing winter gear inside the cramped space.

Flying anywhere this close to the holidays sucked, and I wished that I could've taken another week before returning to the Baranov Family. Oleg Baranov was a demanding boss, but he wouldn't have been that mad if I'd stayed in Moscow a while longer.

It wasn't a matter of pleasing my boss and coming back from a mission on time. It was the need to get back to the expectations I'd had for many years. For two decades, I managed several brothels for Oleg. While the work was good and I'd never have to worry about job security, I hadn't missed it for the last month I'd been gone.

Dread filled me, not excitement. Having a break to go follow a lead on a cold case was a nice change of pace. When Oleg gave an order, I completed it as efficiently as possible. We all did. All the Baranov soldiers knew better than to disobey his instructions. That was why I was still diligent to go to the brothels and keep everything going smoothly. It wasn't passion for the job, but instead, what he wanted me to do.

I heaved out a long sigh, unenthusiastic about having to supervise and deal with the same old shit and drama again.

The older man standing next to me in the line to get out of this terminal chuckled dryly. "It's been an exhausting day, huh?"

I nodded. Small talk wasn't my favorite thing in the world, but I wasn't allergic to it like some of my fellow soldiers and brothers in our Mafia Family. I sure as hell didn't want to pass the time chit-chatting with this dude, though. "Yeah. Sure has," I replied dryly, putting in the bare minimum effort.

"I've got an early day at the office tomorrow." He shook his head slowly, letting his chin dip toward his chest. "That makes it even worse, knowing that as soon as I get out of here and get home, I'll need to just get right back up and deal with the rat race and grind." Glancing at me, he raised his brows. "You know what I mean?"

I nodded again, unable to share details about how I could agree with that, nor was I willing to prolong this conversation.

"Yeah, I know what you mean."

"What business are you in?" he asked. It wasn't a nosy question, but I couldn't answer it.

"Entertainment," I lied. It was partly true and completely none of his business what I did. That was the issue with small talk—it could lead the way to more details being requested.

I pointed to the side, feigning someone looking for me. With that diversion, I could walk out of the bottle-necked mob of this line and get out of answering anything else.

He wouldn't want the truth, that I was just getting back from a month of following old leads about when Oleg's niece, Sonya, disappeared. That tomorrow night, I'd be back to making sure everything went well at the whore houses the law couldn't know about.

Fuck, I don't want to deal with it anymore.

It was all just the same, desperate women and pathetic men who had to pay to get laid. Sure, sex sold, literally. And it was good money, money that made the world go round.

But did *I* have to be the one to run it all? Was this all I'd have to look forward to for the rest of my life?

An hour later, I was in my car and heading through the snow and ice back to the Baranov mansion. Moscow had been wintry too, but somehow, facing it here at home was worse. The brumal winds and blanket of snow seemed to add to the confining sensation of being trapped here.

I could tell him. While it wasn't going against a rule to speak up about a job assignment, it was frowned upon as a rule of thumb. When a man signed up to serve the Boss, that was no light commitment to shrug off. And since I was a distant Baranov by blood, I couldn't shirk my familial duties.

New recruits were screwed, stuck taking whatever he tasked them with. But I'd been around. I wasn't some green, new idiot who needed to be broken into all of this. That was part of the reason Oleg had sent me to Moscow to follow up on the supposed leads. He trusted me, and that was saying something. Not many spoke about Sonya anymore. Most men in the family had forgotten about her, but I recalled her being born and always under the close supervision of her mother, Amelia Baranov.

I'll see what kind of a mood he's in when I mention going back to those houses tomorrow. Perhaps he'd pick up on my lack of interest and inquire about it.

Could I ask him for a reassignment? It felt risky, yet not.

How would that look? Just coming back after being gone and making requests and demands? I didn't want to piss him off, particularly when I would be reporting with no news. Those supposed leads about whatever happened to Sonya ended up being dead ends and nothing more. That wasn't exactly promising news for the man who'd never forgotten about his sister-in-law or niece.

After I arrived at the grand mansion, I parked out front on the circular drive that had recently been plowed and cleared of snow. A short, hurried walk inside brought me to the foyer. I dipped my chin in a nod of acknowledgment to the guards standing to attention, then let myself in to walk further through the house to seek out the Boss.

He'd be in his office and study suite, but I was delayed getting there. Two people waited outside the double doors, and upon seeing them together, I raised my brows high. My mouth hung open, shocked to see one of the Baranovs' deadliest killers making out with Eva Baranov, Oleg's other niece.

"What in the fuck did I miss?" I asked, mostly to myself. The words slipped out of my mouth aloud, though, and even though I spoke quietly, it was enough to prompt them to break apart. Slightly. Lev still held on to her, keeping her within his embrace, almost as if he couldn't bear to take his arms off her and leave her vulnerable to any threat or danger.

"Hey, Vik," Lev greeted, smiling quickly as he tucked Eva to his side. "What's up?"

I blinked. "I could ask you the same thing." I volleyed my gaze back and forth between them. "What is… this?" Eva and I weren't close. We never had any reason to be as distant relatives who shared a surname. I wasn't ever on her security detail since I was delegated to work at the brothels. Still, without knowing everything about the Baranovs' Mafia princess, I knew something significant had to have happened for Lev to feel confident about kissing her like that, in this house.

Eva smiled and stroked her hand down Lev's chest. On her finger, a large diamond ring glittered as it caught the light from the chandelier.

"A lot," Lev answered with a wry laugh. "Since you've been in Moscow, *a lot* has happened. "Eva and I are engaged."

My jaw hung open even more. "Are you serious? You two? How in the hell did that happen?"

"That's a story better told with the Boss," Lev replied.

Eva nodded. "They'll fill you in." Then with another kiss, she began to slip out of his hold. "Welcome back."

"Yeah, sure. Thanks." I ran my hand through my hair and tried to figure out how in the hell Oleg's favorite assassin would be with Eva. She would've been arranged to marry an ally or something, but Lev? There had to be a story there. "And hey, um, congratulations," I said, gesturing at the massive ring on her finger. It had to have been from him, because if this was legit and they were together, she wouldn't cheat on a lethal and seriously dark man like Lev.

"I'll see you later," Lev told Eva as she walked away. He smiled at me, patting my back and shaking my hand as he led the way into Oleg's office. "It's been a busy few months here."

I laughed once. "I was only gone for *one* month."

"And you're always busy at the establishments you supervise."

"Establishments?" I shook my head, grinning. "There's no need to exaggerate."

"Viktor. It is good to see you," Oleg greeted, standing to come welcome me back, cutting off any more talk with Lev.

I shook his hand and accepted his hug, then we moved straight to business. He'd already read through the texts and emails I'd sent him, and the first matter was a little more explanation on my part about why I hadn't received any answers about Sonya in Moscow.

He wasn't disappointed, almost seeming resigned like he accepted that Sonya and her mother were gone from the family. It appeared as though he knew there was nothing we could do about that. It wouldn't prevent him from sending someone to follow supposedly reputable clues and leads, but maybe he only did that out of obligation to never give up on those who were lost.

Instead of moving on to the next topic of business, my expected return to supervising the whore houses, he filled me in on what had happened with Lev and Eva. Lev was assigned as Eva's bodyguard at the huge university, but drama and danger quickly threatened them. Drugs. Rapes. Attacks. All kinds of bad news. It seemed to have all culminated in Eva being taken as bait for the Ilyins to get to Lev.

Between the Petrov Family and the Ilyin Family, someone was vying to have control over the university.

"Rurik is still on campus," Lev said. "But since I was injured—"

"And will soon be marrying Eva," Oleg interjected with a smile, "you, Viktor, are just the man I need to move into position there at the university campus."

"Me?" I didn't point at myself, but I couldn't mask the shock in my one-word reply. Right when I was secretly hoping for a reassignment to anywhere else than the brothels I'd managed for twenty years.

"Yes. You." Oleg nodded, matter-of-fact about it as he folded his hands on top of his desk behind which he sat. "Rurik can stay there and keep up the surveillance. But I can't hold off on following up with the role Irina Petrov plays in this drug war."

Holding back so I wouldn't show too much excitement about not having to go right back to the brothels, I nodded. All business. "Yes, sir. I can do that."

The Boss smiled. "And in order to incorporate you into this project, I think you could very easily fit in on campus."

Lev faced me. "As a professor."

"What?" I laughed once, incredulously. He couldn't be serious. But the sober expression both men wore suggested they meant it. "You want me to…"

"To step in as a temporary professor." Oleg held his hands out as though to imply *why not*. " After all, you do have that degree you never use…"

A degree I'd only obtained through fraud for another case. "That is true." I volleyed my gaze back and forth between them, trying to come up with something else to say.

"I appreciate your flexibility to investigate that slight lead on Sonya in Moscow," Oleg said.

"And we're aware that your place is back at the houses, supervision business as usual," Lev said, sounding more and more like the Boss's right-hand man.

"That's fine, though," I hurried to add. "I don't mind leaving the brothels for someone else to supervise for a while. Honestly, it's been getting old. Wearing on me. The same old, over and over."

Oleg shrugged. "Then it sounds like this is an ideal situation for you, *Professor.*"

I smiled, looking forward to this chance to not have to go back to those whorehouses yet. While I had no clue how playing professor would turn out, I was curious to find out.

2

IRINA

I lingered at the front door to the apartment. Calling it an apartment was an overstatement. This tiny, cramped hovel was barely an excuse for a residence. Yet, it was supposed to be "home" for Maxim. My father put my younger brother here, claiming it was safer for him to live outside the stately Petrov mansion, but he wouldn't fool me. I knew exactly what this grimy apartment was.

It was a prison. A cell. A location where Maxim would never thrive or prosper, like a fugitive.

He'd never done anything wrong—except be born. He'd never acted out or done something to warrant punishment. But here he was, trapped day in and day out, only able to anticipate infrequent visits from me, the only family he had, really. Igor Petrov would rather be dead than acknowledge Maxim as his relative at all.

"Been coming around a lot lately, Irina," the Petrov guard said from his position at the doorway. He arched one graying brow, appearing mildly amused but always bored. This post had to be dull. Expected to keep Maxim here and no visitors in, this guard was nothing more than a glorified babysitter, following my father's decree that Maxim stay out of his sight.

Having grown up surrounded by my father's men, I was used to their talking to me, even challenging me sometimes. I shrugged. "I haven't been on campus since it's winter break," I replied, responding verbally to him at the same time that I signed it out for Maxim. He was deaf, but skilled with reading lips and ASL. I wouldn't agree with this guard that I'd been visiting my brother often. My father only ever allowed me to visit as a hard-earned and seldom-given reward.

"Hmm." The guard nodded. "It's making me wonder if something's going to change around here." He gestured vaguely at the bare, sparsely decorated apartment.

"No changes that I know of," I replied verbally and in ASL. No changes would ever be coming in regard to how Igor Petrov viewed his only son. Maxim had always been less than, and it was because of this that I tried to provide Max with as much nurturing love as I could.

In the corner, near the tiny fake Christmas tree that had yet to be taken down, a small pile of gifts sat for him. I was the one who gave him the minimal luxuries beyond essentials. And even then, I couldn't be guaranteed to know the gifts I bought under my strictly watched allowance would remain with Maxim. My father learned long ago that he could easily punish me by hurting Max and depriving him of nicer things.

"I will see you as soon as I can," I told Max near the door.

He hugged me again, then stepped back to reply with his hands and fingers. "I know you'll be busy in school soon."

My heart ached for his never having that chance. He was still just a teen, a young teen, but the "homeschool" he had and limited online lessons he was permitted here as a deaf and immunocompromised boy weren't the same as the experience of going to school and having the full freedom to learn whatever he wanted to, however he wanted to.

"But I will still visit as soon as I can," I insisted.

He nodded, knowing how things had to be.

For now.

My heart ached as the driver assigned to me grunted in the hallway. "Let's move it."

I was always told what to do, always expected to obey the Petrov men dictating how things would be. I was powerless to help Maxim or demand that he have a better life.

For now.

One day, I would make things better. One day, *someday*, I would take charge of my life and Maxim's.

Behind the driver, I walked out of the filthy apartment building, deadened to the details of such a low quality of life that could be had here. I had to go numb and block it all out. If I didn't, I'd fall prey to the need to scream and rage at the injustice of it all.

For not the first time, I vowed to right this grave wrong. One day, I would kill my father. I would end his life, and in doing so, I would end his power to punish Maxim.

I wouldn't have to be his spy on campus anymore.

I wouldn't be required to report on this drug and turf war he was attempting to not only instigate but win against the Baranovs and the Ilyins, two other prominent Mafia Families in New York.

On the ride back to my father's house, I zoned out and stared unseeing at the scenery as the car sped through the bleak and gray wintry day.

I hated this life. I loathed the details of my existence and prayed I could escape these circumstances—trapped as a daughter, used as a spy, and cast aside as an inferior person who could be as indispensable as the next soldier or guard. It was no *life*. It was a sentence. A curse. A damnation that I was ever so unfortunate to be born a Petrov.

Hating this life was the motivation that fueled me, but declaring freedom from my father was too important of a goal for me to screw it up. I couldn't leave anything to chance. I had to do this correctly, wisely, because if I erred in overthrowing him and robbing him of the power to neglect or punish Maxim, I would risk being a target myself.

The driver took a call, conversing in grunts and one-word sounds. It was all a code, all a ploy to prevent me from actually knowing anything of use.

Again, I was used to it. But witnessing another call designed to keep information from me reiterated how careful I would need to be when I killed my father and ended his reign of terror—the terror over me and Maxim.

I couldn't count on any of the Petrov men to surrender or turn rat. I couldn't look to any allies within the Petrov Family to assist me or even offer advice. Wishful thinking had me dreaming of asking some of the men to help me stage a coup. None would be willing, though, as all of them, young and old, feared Igor. Younger soldiers were too naïve to act out, eager to win the favor of the bosses and leaders within the organization. Older soldiers were too content and comfortable in their seniority to rebel.

No, it would be up to *me*, up to me alone to save myself and Maxim. As soon as I could strategize a plan to end my father, I would do so on my terms. I had to escape without a trace and ensure no one would hunt me and Maxim down without the rule of my father in place.

The drive back to my father's house didn't take that long. As usual, the ride there seemed too short. For all my twenty-three years of life, I'd been a pawn in his schemes. I'd been expected to do as he said, existing with a short leash.

Unwilling to exit the car and go into the house, I stared out the window for a few seconds too long. Daring to daydream that I were anywhere else, I tuned out the sound of the driver getting out and closing his door, the sight of him walking around to open my door. He wasn't moving out of chivalry or to be a gentleman. He was nothing more than another ward seeing to my imprisonment.

With the door open and the cold air hitting my face, I shivered. Yet, I couldn't will my body to move. I didn't want to see my father's face. I didn't want to hear his ugly voice.

"Get out," the driver ordered, glaring down at me.

I did, with a resigned sigh, as I left the peace of the car to head inside.

My father was waiting for me, no doubt annoyed that I'd insisted on seeing Maxim today. He saw every visit as a waste of time. According to him, all my time should be spent catering to his needs, to whatever my father decided was necessary for me to do or concern myself about.

Over the last few days, those awkward ones between the winter holidays when nothing seemed to go on as usual, he'd been busy on the phone and holding meetings. Today, though, he seemed to be prepared to catch up with me.

"Sit." From his perch on one of the antique chairs in the biggest living room, he pointed at the sofa. His face remained lined, both from wrinkles and a scowl. Nothing about his visage suggested any paternal love or care. Here, like this, I was just one employee among many, apparently failing to please him.

I sat, used to perfecting my mask of indifference. On my face, he would see nothing. No fear. No excitement. No love. Not even a need to please or willingness to do my duty.

"What have you learned from the Baranov bitch?" His tone was cutting and impatient, like it always was.

"Nothing."

His scowl deepened. "Nothing?"

"I haven't spoken to Eva since the semester ended." He wouldn't get a rise out of me. I was telling the truth. I hadn't spoken to Eva Baranov since I helped her and her bodyguard lover, Lev, escape. My father had teamed up with the Ilyins to have Lev captured. It was all a complicated series of lies and maneuvers, but I declared myself a traitor when I gave Eva a small file to cut the bindings holding her in place. I went against my father's duplicitous intentions when I told her how to get out of that warehouse.

Those truths would never be shared with Igor Petrov, though. I would take that deception to the grave.

I was *glad* that Eva was safe—not because we were friends but because I hated how my father would attempt to ruin everyone's lives without a care.

He shot to his feet, though, furious. "The Ilyins are pissed about how this all ended. They blame *me* for the fact that Lev got away. That the Baranov girl escaped."

Of course, the rival family would be mad at him. He'd tried to con them by pretending to help set up the capture. I crossed my arms and said nothing.

He wasn't done lashing out, though, stalking toward me and hunching over. Thrusting his pointed finger at me, he narrowed his eyes and glowered at me. "I swear, Irina, if you helped her, if you had any part in how they got away, I *will* find out."

I refused to react, not letting him see any fear or worry. I couldn't in this game of power and punishment. If he suspected I'd helped the enemies get free, he'd dole out his punishment on Maxim, not me.

Because my father knew how to hit where it hurt the most, and that was in seeing to Maxim's pain and suffering.

"You are my daughter, Irina." Straightening from his slant, he puffed out his chest and looked down his big, ruddy nose at me. "You are my daughter."

Tell me something I don't know, asshole.

"You are my spy. My servant in this family."

I hate you.

He lifted his head higher, to emulate a more regal stance as he viewed me. "You are mine to do with as I please. In all ways. You are mine to order as I see fit." Grinning in a malicious snarl, he added, "And that is all you'll ever be."

Keeping my narrow gaze on him, I promised that wouldn't be true.

You're wrong. You have to be wrong.

Until I could kill him and be free, he could assume that. For now, though, while I could vow to kill him and sever his control someday, I only had the immediate future to look forward to.

I can't wait to get back to school. Back on campus. He only ever sent me there to spy on the drug business he was setting up. But it would also be a break from being in this house with him, a pause from having to live with him and put up with him day in and day out when my heart longed for the freedom of another life—one where no one would ever use me as a pawn.

3

VIKTOR

I went to college back when I was younger and not as used to the harder aspects of what it meant to be a Baranov soldier. Oleg had asked me to consider a business degree, or even a law degree. Some needs of the family could be varied like that. Ultimately, he asked me to oversee a mission at one of the whorehouses, though, and that was that. I ended my college courses after only a year and had been stuck at the brothels ever since.

It almost felt like a full circle to come back to a college campus now. This was where I had been before my career with the business of sex, and it was where I was returning now.

Nothing was the same. I assumed nothing would be the same since I'd last been on a campus twenty years ago. But that wasn't something I couldn't figure out how to deal with. Any mission, even unexpected, out-of-the-blue ones that popped up like Oleg's request for me to go to Moscow and follow those old clues about Sonya, could warrant drastic adjustments. As spies for the Boss, we employed disguises. In order to look like a professor, I shifted my appearance to a cleaner cut, with a professionally acceptable suit and tie, but I took care not to look too stuffy or formal. Also in the name of being a spy or operative, we used aliases, which was why I was here as Professor Viktor Remi, not Viktor Baranov. I'd need to tidy up my language and adopt a whole different personality to fit in here.

All of those changes were doable. Even though I was usually in supervision at the whorehouses, I was still up to the challenge of altering myself for the job.

When I arrived, both to check out my office on campus and my apartment nearby, I couldn't help but look at everything as though it were all new. As if I had never been a college student. It would've been smarter to view it all with the mindset that I belonged here as a fraudulent professor. Keeping the facts straight was critical in any mission, but the more I meandered around campus and realized it was much bigger than I had given it credit for, I saw it as what it could've been. If Oleg had decided so long ago that I'd serve more of a purpose with a different career in the family, I wouldn't have had to endure so long at the whorehouses and deal with so many morons. The family had a vast amount of wealth, and it all came from Oleg's smart choices in diversifying our income. My role here to spy on the drug trade and turf issues was just one more facet of ensuring we stayed prime like that.

Rurik met up with me, more familiar with the campus and ready to fill me in on more than what Oleg and Lev had told me at the Baranov mansion and headquarters.

The tall man was dressed for the weather, wearing a thick coat and keeping his hands shoved in his pockets. Atop his head was navy beanie, and if I didn't know better, he could've resembled a student, not a man much older and deadlier than many others here.

"How's it going, man?" I greeted, accepting his handshake and pat on the back. I wondered how long he'd been waiting in the parking lot for me.

"Cold," he answered wryly but honestly. He gestured for me to start down a path leading to the east. Since he'd come here when Lev started as Eva's bodyguard, he'd served the role of being a backup guard, eyes and ears for Lev when he couldn't get away to follow up on what any Petrov or Ilyin men were doing on campus. As we walked toward the building where the English department was housed—since I was here to fake being a professor of American English History—he caught me up on how the Baranov presence started here.

Lev came to follow Eva around because she'd wanted a taste of being a "normal" twentysomething. She befriended a woman named Kelly, and even though the two were supposed to have been roommates, they'd only become friends, close to the point that they snuck out to a party and witnessed some sketchy things. From following Eva and Kelly for the majority of the fall semester last year, both Rurik and Lev gathered more information about how drugs were being distributed at a higher rate, even though no one could really tell who was selling them and where they were coming from. Rapes and attacks on women had also gone up. Eva had almost been raped at a party by a member from a rival family, and Kelly had been drugged and might have been attacked.

"You don't know?" I asked Rurik. He seemed awfully familiar with details about Kelly.

"No. We couldn't tell. After Kelly was found unconscious in the shower room, she more or less moved in with Eva and Lev at their apartment off campus."

"More or less?" I asked, curious about that detail and how he'd worded it. She either did or didn't move in. Regardless, it sounded like Ms. Kelly Garnet had been approved by someone higher up to receive security under the umbrella of protection an association with the Baranov name could deliver on.

"Kelly moved in for a while, but before the end of the semester, she left again."

I furrowed my brow, blinking at the light snow falling and dropping into my eyes as we walked. "Could she be working against the family? Getting close to spy?"

He shook his head but didn't seem bothered by my question. Being that paranoid was just a given.

"No. She had no ties with anyone else in the Mafia. She came from a difficult background, but Lev ran extensive checks on her."

He continued updating me on what he'd noticed in his on-and-off-again surveillance on campus. Over the winter break, with so many students gone home or not at school, everything stalled and died down. With the next semester starting again, he anticipated more activity from any returning Petrov and Ilyin men on campus.

"I appreciate your giving me the rundown," I told him as we walked into the large, old building that housed the English department.

"No problem. I look forward to working with you again."

We hadn't crossed paths regularly, but we were brothers, regardless.

"I'm not surprised that the Boss wanted someone else to come in on this. Lev is busy with Eva. And after the way they escaped, I can't blame them for wanting some distance from all of this," he added.

"Sounds like a reassignment was necessary."

He glanced at me, brushing the snow off the top of his hat. "But I am surprised that you'd give up your position at the, uh…" Looking around at the few people in the hallway, he cleared his throat.

"Establishments," I suggested as a cleaner alternative for *brothels* in case anyone was listening in on what we said. The family's whorehouses were certainly not legal places of commerce.

"Yes. I'm surprised you'd be interested in giving up time working at the establishments to come here."

I shrugged, keeping an eye on the students and staff-like people in the halls. "I got tired of it."

Rurik laughed once, smirking at me. "Tired of the, um, professionals there?" A salacious grin covered his face.

I nodded. He wouldn't understand. Sure, in the beginning, it was fun and adventurous being surrounded by elite whores and dancers. After twenty years of it, it was all the same old. Nothing new. I'd seen enough tits and pussies that the novelty of it all had soured.

"Yeah. Basically," I answered. "Going to and coming back from Moscow wasn't enough of a break from it. I'm glad to do something different for a while, get back into the field, so to speak."

Rurik laughed again. "Even if it means grading papers?"

I shrugged. "Yeah. Why not?" Grading papers and making up lessons would go a long way to making this experience different. It would be tedious busywork, but that sounded like a nice change of pace. If doing those things would make my presence here as a professor that much more believable, then that was what I'd put up with.

We continued down the massive corridor to reach my office, but it wasn't a simple stroll. Countless women watched us, all checking me—or Rurik—out. I felt their stares burning, but it didn't matter. None of them would matter. They all looked way too inexperienced—in a bad way, not a sexy one. I never cared too much about a woman's age when I wanted to get laid, but something about these academic ones just made them *too* young.

Rurik left me at the door to my office, agreeing that we'd be in touch more often on campus, working together. He was expected to just keep an eye on everything, being the eyes and ears, but I was expected to follow up on Irina Petrov more closely. She'd be a student in my lecture hall. Giving lectures would be different, but I was up for it. It was all the more reason to familiarize myself with the material. If I were extra prepared and confident in acting like a professor, I would have more energy and time to devote to watching her both in my class and outside of it, when I could.

Settling into my office wouldn't take long. I just wanted to get acquainted with what went where. Oleg's hackers had already handled the headache of putting me into the system here, but still, getting around in the computer system required a few minutes of my attention.

When my stomach growled, reminding me that I had yet to get lunch, I logged out of half of the things I had open on my laptop. I'd leave soon. I could go to my apartment and order something to be delivered there. Before I could make good on my plan to leave, a tall, gorgeous redhead knocked on my door that I'd left cracked open a couple of inches.

"Hey, there," she greeted with a sexy purr that would've been more fitting at my previous job. "I thought I saw someone come in here." She entered fully, giving me a full look of her svelte figure, huge tits, and flawless face. A coy, confident smile lifted her lips, but it seemed too cunning for me to ever lower my guard. "You must be Professor Remi. Viktor, right?" She increased the wattage of her smile, extending her hand for me to shake it. "I'm Jessica Nolan, assistant director of administration."

And you just happened to be here? Her title sounded like something that would be found in the main administrative offices.

"Nice to meet you," I lied. I didn't need to know anything else about this woman to realize she was an opportunist, horny and eager to fuck her way anywhere. Women only gazed at men the way she did when they wanted dick.

"Oh, nice to meet you, too," she replied, proving my point when she faked stumbling over her own foot and falling into me. Leaning forward, she practically thrust her tits into my face. "Whoops."

"You all right?"

She was slow to stand upright again, running her hand over my shoulder and squeezing. "I'd be even better if you took me out to dinner tonight. I would love to personally welcome you onboard."

Yeah, no thanks. That's enough of that.

"No." I shook my head. "I'm not interested in a personal welcome. I'm here to work, Ms. Nolan, and that's it."

"Oh." She huffed as if I were being silly. "Just Jessica, please. Are you sure I can't interest you in anything else?" She dipped her chin, giving me a sex-kitten look.

"I'm sure." I wasn't falling for this bullshit. Of course, sleeping with someone for intel wasn't out of the question, but this woman wasn't a person of interest.

Jessica was quick to change her tune, pouting—and even that was sexy, but annoying. "Are you *really* sure? Because I'm the dean's niece." She set her hands on the desk, slanting over so I'd get a full view of her low-cut dress revealing the tops of her breasts. "And I'm *really* used to getting my way."

I tilted my head to the side. "Is that a threat?" I could play hardball if I had to. I didn't want this woman trying to bother me, but I wasn't going to ruin a connection I might need later.

"Oh, no." She beamed at me. "Just making myself clear."

That you intend to prey on me. Great. "Noted." I nodded to further acknowledge her and how easy she wanted to make herself seem.

As she left my office, I sat there and wondered if I'd have more complications than I expected in taking this job.

The goal was clear. The Boss's instructions were simple.

Get close to Irina Petrov and obtain whatever intel I could.

Getting close to any other woman wasn't on the agenda.

4

IRINA

The first day of the spring semester was here. I'd spent every day leading up to it at my father's house, holed up in my room unless he demanded I attend dinner with him. Those meals were only more opportunities for him to berate me, remind me that I was nothing, or order me not to try to mess around when the semester started. Having my only parent tell me that I was useless unless I was gathering intel for him was a hell of a downer.

I wasn't allowed to have a dorm room anymore, not since someone had gone to the room that Eva and Kelly Garnet were supposed to share. Eva hadn't lived on campus, staying with Lev elsewhere. But Kelly had been in the dorms.

After stopping by the apartment adjacent to the campus—which therefore made it feel like it was part of campus, after all—I headed toward my first building. The morning was crisp and chilly, the kind of low temperature that made the air seem to turn to ice and crystalize in your lungs if you took too deep of a breath.

"I can't wait for summer," I mumbled under my breath, my mouth hidden by my scarf as I walked to the coffee shop so I could order a hot drink on the way to my first lecture.

No one heard me. No guards were nearby. They were always present, someone on campus, but my father chose not to have a bodyguard on me all the time. If he arranged for that kind of security detail, it would alienate me as someone others wouldn't trust or talk to, and that would defeat the purpose of my gathering intel. On another note, he probably didn't give a shit about me and whether I were to ever get hurt. I had a purpose for him, and I served as an asset for his plans, but that never meant he cared about *me*.

While the Petrov guards were always here somewhere, giving me some distance but keeping an eye on me, I appreciated how they stayed back. I would go insane if I couldn't vent my complaints sometime, in some way.

Summer was my favorite season, and I wanted to be stupidly optimistic that I could be free by then. That "someday" would come before summer arrived and I could make good on my vow to kill my father and not have to worry about my father hurting Maxim anymore.

In the coffee shop, I got in line and unwrapped my scarf so I could breathe clearer. Sucking in a deep inhale of the aromatic scent of coffee beans being ground and brewed, I closed my eyes and tried to calm down from the stress of the last few weeks. Igor Petrov was a stressor of the highest degree.

When I opened my eyes, I blinked them again in surprise. Standing in front of me in line was a familiar head of blonde hair. She wore a beanie, but still, the long, golden waves splayed over her shoulders.

Kelly Garnet was only important to me as someone close to Eva Baranov, who had been a person of interest for my father. Since seeing Kelly in the health clinic on campus after she was drugged, though, I couldn't help but wonder about how she was doing. I had also been at the health clinic at that time, when one of my "friends" had been attacked. At that time, the socialite I'd pretended to befriend had started a rumor that Eva was the link to why so many more and more potent drugs were circulating on campus. Those girls weren't ever my friends. I only let them think they were close to me for the sake of looking somewhat popular and outgoing so others would loosen up around me.

I tapped her shoulder gently, smiling as she turned to face me. "Hey, Kelly."

She raised her brows, slowly looking me up and down. No obvious recognition showed on her face, but I knew she remembered me. She couldn't fake it. I pointed at myself anyway, kind of lamely. "Irina?"

Kelly nodded, cool as a cucumber. "I remember."

Awkward silence hung between us after that. I couldn't accept that this was it. Yeah, her alliance would lie with Eva, but that couldn't mean she'd never tolerate small talk with me.

"You're looking good."

Actually, she wasn't. She looked tired. If stressed had a look, she was wearing it.

Her reply was a simple, short nod.

I wouldn't be deterred. "How have you been feeling after..." I looked around to see if anyone was listening in. "After you were drugged?"

"Fine." Kelly looked ahead to gauge how the line was moving. This aloof thing was either a well-rehearsed act or she was not in the mood to speak to me.

Still, I wasn't a quitter. "How is Eva doing?"

Now she reacted. She narrowed her eyes slightly, getting defensive at the mention of her friend. Or former friend. Eva wasn't here anymore, so it was a guessing game whether the Baranov princess was still in touch with this "commoner".

When she turned again, facing forward and literally giving me her back, I furrowed my brow. Feigning ignorance, I acted as though she hadn't heard me. "Kelly? How's Eva?"

Glancing at me with an icy smirk, she shook her head. "Look elsewhere if you're on the hunt for gossip."

Dammit. She not only knew who I was but she also recalled that I had interacted with Eva before. And I had been near others who'd spread rumors about Eva, all for the purpose of getting Lev to come out for my father's men to capture him.

Now I gave up. I stopped trying to get a rise out of her, or any answers. She clearly wasn't giving me any.

Besides, I didn't need Kelly to tell me how Eva was doing. I'd asked mostly out of curiosity whether Kelly and Eva were still talking to each other. Whether others would view Kelly as a source of leverage against the Baranovs because of her association with Eva.

It was common knowledge through the Mafia families that Eva was safe and staying off campus. She was committed with Lev. She lived at the Baranov residence again, untouchable and out of reach.

After I ordered my drink, I waited in line and thought back to when I first noticed that Eva had the hots for Lev. He was always near her, always within reach. It started as smoldering looks that I doubted they realized they couldn't hide. Then it evolved into more knowing expressions, like they were crappy at keeping their attraction a secret. I couldn't blame her. He wasn't hard on the eyes. Tall, muscular, and so dangerous.

I'd never experienced that sort of attraction for a man. First of all, I never had the freedom to want a man or get to know someone for the exclusive purpose of dating. So long as my father ruled my life, I wouldn't be able to experience something as ordinary as that.

More so, I'd never felt such a connection with a guy. No attraction. No love-at-first sight just looking at a man and the vision of him making me gaga for him. No swift realization of the presence of a handsome man stealing my breath.

I especially never felt any such attraction for the Petrov guards on my father's staff. I had to routinely do my best not to grimace at them with disgust, bothered by them on an elemental level because they supported my father no matter what, blindly doing as he said. That was the way of Mafia families. The big boss called the shots, and everyone followed. But when the boss was a sadistic asshole who'd scorned his own flesh and blood, where was the mercy or justice in that? I hadn't asked to be born a Petrov.

All the guards who worked for the Petrov Family were old and gross. The younger ones were too full of themselves and indoctrinated with the idea that I was a bratty burden to deal with because that was how my father projected me to be.

Besides, I *always* had to watch what I said around them. Friendship was out of the question, too. It had to be. I was unable to lower my guard and slip. Letting them know how much I hated my father would be the first grievance that would make him overly suspicious of me.

There's no hope, anyway. If I couldn't find the courage and know-how to take out my father, he'd arrange me in a marriage I wouldn't want. Mafia bosses were notorious for picking who would be their sons-in-law, another method of transacting business and making deals.

I sipped my drink the rest of the way toward the huge building where my first class would be held. If I could fake interest in any of the classes I took, this one would be easy. English was my first love, and combining history with it made it even better.

I chose my classes randomly, though, never permitted to assume all this time here would amount to a degree.

With such low spirits, reminded as always that I would have no say of anything in my life until I killed my father, I sighed and continued down the wide corridor. A poster hung behind a glass case caught my eye.

I paused, sipping my coffee and relishing the burn of the coffee down my throat. It almost thawed me out from the walk here.

Inside the case was a graphic illustration for a Nancy Drew book. The department was running a theme on the series, and I smiled at the comforting scene that covered the first book of that collection. Maxim and I loved mysteries, and I'd lost count of how many times I'd read that book to him. It was a favorite, one I'd read with him on my lap when he was younger. He'd feel the vibration of me talking and read along.

Oh, Max. I shook my head as I carried on toward the hall entrance, hating for the nth time that my younger brother had to suffer from the one and only diabolical mind of Igor Petrov. Our father was a bastard of the highest order to ever try to punish him just because he was deaf and weak. He was the devil himself for ever trying to hurt his child. For ever using me in a game against his well-being.

As I stepped inside the hall, I glanced down at the solitary man standing on the stage where the podium stood for the lecturer.

In this case, the professor of American English History.

Specifically, the extremely sexy brute of a man, looking so dapper and dashing in a black button-up and slacks, a bold red tie hanging from his neck.

Oh. Whoa.

I paused with my coffee cup midway to my mouth. I couldn't swallow even if I tried right now. My mouth was dry. Yet, my heart raced and my breath quickened.

Never say never...

Because looking at my new professor, I felt that lightning bolt of lust strike me down, rendering me speechless as I checked out a man I definitely would have *no* right to want.

5

VIKTOR

Students filed into the lecture hall. The mass of men and women displayed a variety—young and old, sophisticated and sloppy, all shapes and sizes. If the university didn't put a lot of emphasis on catering to a diverse group, it would be a surprise. Then again, it might've just been representative of how highly sought-after this university was, even if it was borderline considered Ivy League.

One thing that remained consistent across all the people entering the cavernous auditorium was how they perceived *me*.

More than a few checked me out with interest that burned hotter and lasted longer than scoping out who their new professor was. So many of the women seemed so damn young, childish and too immature to even be here where adults were supposed to learn and prepare for a career.

It was a stark difference from what I was used to. Before I was tasked with going to Moscow to follow the leads about Sonya, I saw older women, experts who could manipulate a man and then fuck them ten ways to hell. Prostitutes and dancers. Those were the kinds of women who were more my speed. I'd tired of that speed, and I was grateful for a break from going back to the whorehouses to supervise there, but it didn't diminish the stark contrast to what I'd see here.

I waited at the podium, not smiling but not scowling either. Without revealing what kind of a prof I would be, I scanned the throngs of students entering for the face of Irina Petrov, the one person I was supposed to pay attention to and follow the best that I could.

And there she was. At last.

There she was.

Tall. Slender. Straight chestnut hair hanging down over her shoulders. Light blue eyes that sparkled despite the distance yawning between us as she delicately walked down the aisle. She sought a seat, not looking up at me once. Placing her high leather boots over the carpeted aisle that directed down toward me at the base of this room, she emitted the aura and confidence of a woman who knew exactly what she wanted. Cool, collected, and poised.

God. Damn...

I huffed out a long breath, needing to vent the pent-up feelings that bottled up in me so suddenly. My first look of this woman shocked me, rendering me slightly awed by her beauty. Sure, she looked young. I knew from her file that she was only twenty-three. She *was* young, but unlike the rest of the students in here, she exuded an old-soul kind of maturity.

I'd counted on her being elegant, a woman used to the finer things in life and within the means of affording any beauty product, any hairstyle, and any designer garments.

But the utter sexiness in her graceful stride distracted me. The slender curves of her definitely non-childish figure gave me pause.

It was the attitude in her haughty pose and lift of her chin that had me wanting to smile.

She was no meek Mafia princess. She wouldn't be a peer of Eva.

This woman, my target to spy on, would be a challenge.

And I couldn't wait to pursue her.

Even though she didn't look up at me once as she chose a seat and sat in it, I was aware that I'd have my work cut out for me. She wouldn't make this easy. She wouldn't be cooperative. I could guess it in the simple consideration of her regal posture and the almost stern press of her lips.

I couldn't single her out—yet. Right now, I had to focus on establishing my cover as a professor, and that meant beginning this first class. Fortunately, this distraction by Irina's beauty wouldn't hinder me from pulling that off. First days of classes were usually nothing more than a prolonged hello and welcome to the course. Reading off and paraphrasing the syllabus was often the norm for day one, and I hadn't even spent much time collecting the material for the syllabus. Reusing what the previous professor had left behind had made it an easy, streamlined chore.

Everyone in the room settled into their seats to peer down at me. Once the collective silence turned into a simmering patience for something to happen, I cleared my throat. Tearing my gaze from the spot where Irina was seated was a conscious effort I had to focus on.

"Welcome to American English History." I looked around at the sea of faces, determined not to give Irina any particular interest. Letting my awareness of her be too obvious would be a grave mistake, and I was more seasoned than that.

She couldn't recognize *me*, not when I'd spent so much of my time as a Baranov soldier and member of the family behind the scenes, at the whorehouses and not "in circulation" as other soldiers and guards she might have seen before. Likewise, this was the first time I'd spotted her in person, versus in a photo.

"I'm Professor Remi, and I'll be starting this semester off with a preview of my expectations for the course."

Was I speaking with a dry, monotone effort? Yes. Did I care? No. If they all perceived me as an unfun professor, it didn't matter. I wasn't here to win any awards. I was here to do my job and do it well.

Starting the lesson with an overview of the syllabus was a boring way to kick things off. It was obvious that the students weren't enthusiastic about what I said. Listing out class rules, bulleting the expectations on assignments, and reviewing the grading rubric, I bored them all to death. Still, as I spoke, the shine of lust didn't dim from all the women watching me.

All of them—except Irina.

Throughout my spiel, she didn't give me a direct look once. Her deliberate avoidance of making eye contact couldn't be a mistake or a fluke.

But why? She couldn't know I was a Mafia man. So why would she be this recalcitrant to facing me, just one of many professors here on campus?

Then she slipped. She broke her stubbornness not to look at me, not to give me attention. With one glance, she peered at me, almost lifting her lips in an expression of annoyed disapproval.

Aha. There was my proof that she had something against me.

What is it? She doesn't like being told what to do, and hearing my reading of the syllabus reminded her that she had to deliver on expectations?

Why's she so cool toward me? Even if I wasn't giving a boring lecture, she could regard me with a basic lack of interest, not something like sassy irritation. Other students looked halfway asleep but they didn't almost glare at me.

The longer I droned on, the more my mind wandered. She was my focus, and it didn't take much energy or creativity on my part to start to fantasize about making her lose that attitude.

Would she scowl and lash out if I tried to kiss that smirk on her face? Or would she pull me closer and want more?

Would she push me away and fight me back if I tried to haul her over my lap and spank her ass red? Or would she moan and wiggle against me for something harder?

Fuck. I couldn't let myself get carried away. I couldn't keep thinking about her like this. If I did, I'd get hard, and I doubted that would be a stellar image on my first day of being a professor here, even if I'd gotten here by fraudulent means.

As I finished up, summarizing the assignment of what would need to be read and reviewed before next week's class, I glanced up and checked the class's reactions.

The second I caught her rolling her eyes, I paused.

Oh, that sass... Once more, I was intrigued.

She muttered something under her breath, something only for her ears to hear. But the sight of her plump lips moving was enough for me to narrow my eyes.

"What's that?" I asked.

Putting her on the spot was a deviation from how I'd handled this lecture so far. I hadn't asked a student anything. I hadn't spoken to anyone directly.

Until now.

She pushed me, though, and I waited calmly for her to answer me.

"Excuse me?" she asked. Her thin brows arched in a silent question.

"What did you say?" I asked again, stern and without any nonsense in my tone.

She sat up, lifting her chin higher. "I remarked about your misuse of contractions on your slide."

LEONA WHITE

I turned, glancing at the slide on the screen that showed what I was reading and summarizing with a hefty dose of bullshitting my way through it all.

"You're, as in you are, not your, the possessive," she explained.

I wanted to parrot her immature gesture of rolling my eyes. I didn't make this material. I recycled it from whoever taught this class before. But I refrained.

"I applaud you for paying close attention," I told her without emotion, keeping up this boring professor act, "but I would suggest you devote more of it toward the substance of the lessons than the delivery of the slides provided by other faculty members."

No one liked a grammar nerd, but I refused to let her try to look like she was schooling *me*.

Challenge accepted, sweetheart.

"Then perhaps you could consider the suggestion that you review the material you copy and paste before sharing it," she replied.

Several students smiled and laughed lightly, appreciating this criticism and that she talked back.

While I didn't think she was doing this for attention or to be a class clown, I recognized that she might want to act out as a way of rebelling.

That's even better. I looked forward to a chance to tame her.

"I'll be keeping a close eye on you," I warned, still not letting any emotions leak into my reply.

She didn't react, only staring at me coolly.

Mark my words. I really would be keeping a close eye on her. Even though she had the presence of Petrov guards nearby—the pair of older men I'd spotted in my peripheral when they glanced in through the open doors at the back of the hall—I would keep Irina Petrov close in my mind and sight.

Now that I could look forward to the thrill of a challenge with getting closer to her, I let myself enjoy a dash of excitement about my reassignment here.

All in the name of getting intel for the Boss, of course.

Nothing more, no matter how sexy of a challenge she might be.

6

IRINA

How was *he* a professor?

The question stuck with me long after I left that lecture. Spotting such a sexy man at the podium had thrown me off. It wasn't just that he was so hot, so attractive that he'd literally stolen my breath. More than anything, my uneasiness and lack of mental equilibrium was due to how he'd put me on the spot, calling *me* out, only me, among the hundred-plus students in that lecture hall.

I'd tried my damnedest not to look at him, certainly not when he could notice. I was a pro at masking my emotions, dammit. I was no amateur at hiding my feelings and making sure no one could ever claim that they could read me.

I had to. Developing this skill was critical when I had to live with Igor Petrov and constantly be his spy. This wasn't a hobby or pastime. I'd furthered this ability to look blank and unaffected because it was the only way I could get through the life I was stuck with.

"Not again," I grumbled as I headed out of the women's locker room at the biggest and best gym on campus.

Not freaking again.

There he was. Professor Remi. He just had to come to this gym, at this hour. I'd never believed in coincidences, but if this wasn't one, fate was throwing me a hell of a curveball to ensure I would encounter the sexy professor every which way I turned and looked!

It'd be easier to avoid him if he didn't happen to be everywhere I went. It would be a manageable feat to prevent making eye contact if he didn't show up on campus.

I saw him in the hallways in the building where English and theology classes were taught. Passing him by left me with a lingering sensation of a burn after his glare on me.

I saw him eating at my favorite café on campus. Trying to ignore his presence might have been possible if he hadn't chosen the table directly across from me.

I saw him working on something in the grand library, jotting notes. Failing to remember a single line of the geology text I was trying to study was a moment of frustration.

Every. Freaking. Where. If the man wasn't following me, something was up for him to constantly be near me like this. And he couldn't have been following me. I would've known if he were. While my father's guards kept a consistent distance from me, they were there. And they weren't untrained idiots. If anyone was actively stalking me, they'd know, and they'd report on it.

As far as I could tell, Professor Remi was just... a professor. Dry, cool, emotionless, but so fine to gaze at. Particularly as he went through a series of reps near the free weight area. I was a "lazy" athlete, doing the bare minimum of a jog on a treadmill and dabbling with some calisthenic type moves that were probably actually Pilates maneuvers.

His muscles bulged and tensed as he lifted then lowered the dumbbells. When he moved on to the machines, more of his tendons and veins popped up and showed.

Compared to the younger men exercising around him, students my age, he looked so damn mature. Older, but not ancient. Powerful, but not hyped up on steroids and protein powder substitutes.

Professor Remi, whoever the hell he was beneath the icy demeanor and no-nonsense style of lecturing, was hot, buff, and experienced. Even in the gym, as he moved from one thing to another, it was so evident that he was a man at ease with his body, with his strength.

This man was no newbie. He wasn't playing around and passing time. He was here to do business, and I couldn't stop admiring his confidence and experience.

I couldn't stop admiring him at all—until I had to. Mid-rep, he glanced up and made direct eye contact with me through the reflections in the mirror.

Caught staring, I couldn't look away. Doing so would prove that he'd caught me. All I could manage was maintaining this eye contact, running on the treadmill and locking in on this blank expression so he wouldn't know how much I lusted for him.

You bastard. You teasing bastard.

Not lowering his gaze as he lifted the dumbbell, he stared right back, trying to play my game of indifference. Or maybe it wasn't indifference on his part. Maybe he really did loathe me and want me to see that almost-scowl of annoyance on his face.

Our stare-down only ended when a couple of girls approached him, asking him stupid, mindless questions about what he'd covered in our last class. Twice, I'd sat through his lectures, and twice, I'd had to refrain from rolling my eyes at the inane questions some of my classmates asked all so he would look at them and speak to them directly. That was how desperate they were to get his attention, how deeply he could distract the entire class from focusing on lessons.

Try as I might, I couldn't shake the sexy prof from my mind when he showed up everywhere I went. Even off campus.

At the end of the second week of classes, I got word of a party happening at an apartment off campus. Parties weren't my thing. They could *look* like my idea of fun, but I hated them. Going to any social events always came with the caveat that I'd be a spy for my father. Or I'd be a diversion for him while he carried on a meeting with a rival. I'd never attended a gathering or social event purely for the sake of just being there. In the same vein that I had to make "friends" for the sake of blending in and pretending to fit in so people would talk to me, I had to force myself into situations where others could think they were partying.

No matter where I went and what I was doing, it always had to serve a purpose for my father.

Tonight was no exception. After getting word that a man who dealt drugs would be hosting a party, I knew I had to go. So far, I wasn't getting anything to report to my father. And he would ask. He would demand a report on what was happening on the drug front at campus. He would expect me to tell him what members of rival families were doing at the school.

And to date, I had nothing to tell him. Kelly wouldn't say anything about Eva, and even if she hadn't been closed-lipped and told me something, I'd fudge those details to make the "news" sound relevant. I wouldn't go out of my way to save her. I wasn't that much of a martyr, except where Maxim was concerned, but I wouldn't let my father have any more intel about Eva or Lev. They deserved their happiness.

Maybe something will happen at this party and I'll have something for him.

Even if it was just the usual same old of people buying and selling, the known users and dealers who'd already made their identities known on campus, it would be a nugget of intel.

For the first hour, as I had a beer and mingled and danced with a couple of outgoing girls I knew from a few of my classes, I realized I might have jinxed myself. Nothing was happening. This party—if it could be called that—was really low-key. Boring, even. Uneventful. Yet, I was glad I'd come to do my part and spy. If I didn't, and if Igor thought I was slacking, he'd punish Maxim.

"Funny seeing *you* here."

I whipped around, nearly dropping my half-full beer bottle at the sound of that rich, gruff voice so close to my ear. I hated that I recognized it already after just two classes. I detested how my body reacted to the thought of *him* being so close to me.

Sure enough, as I completed a spin and faced him, I was treated—or cursed—to the close-up view of Professor Remi. Viktor Remi, according to the scant bio on the college's website.

"Oh?" I pretended to sip my drink, refusing to let him see how surprised I was to see him here. "How come?"

He stepped closer to me as a couple of people danced behind him. That minor closeness felt like both a threat and a lure. This much nearer to him, I was trapped under the hit of his body heat, the taunt of his cologne.

Oh, fuck.

I was almost flush against him, and for the first time in my life, I worried my mask would slip. That he'd see how much he affected me.

"I've been suffering from a specific optical illusion lately." He lifted his drink—not beer but liquor, proving again that he was an older, wiser, and more experienced man versus these beer-loving frat boys—and set his lips on the rim. I was beholden to stare, locked in watching him swallow the liquid. Gazing at his mouth and wondering what else he could do with it heated me up. Desire flooded me as I wondered if he would also be a different lover compared to the men on campus. Older, wiser, and more experienced to rock my world and kiss me everywhere I could dream of.

Stop! Snap out of it! I furrowed my brow, hating how much he got to me. "What kind of an illusion?" I asked, proud that my voice was as cool and chilly as ever.

"An illusion of you—showing up everywhere I fucking look, Ms. Petrov."

I damn near shivered. Not only at his smoky, deep voice, but that he'd cursed. That his eyes narrowed with spite as he complained about seeing me. How? How could I be turned on? How could this… tension building between us be such a lethal turn-on?

"What is wrong with me?" I asked it. I didn't only wonder it, but I lost my control over the moment to the point that I *asked* him. I didn't want to know why he was peeved with me. I didn't need to know the reason he'd caused me to feel like this. He couldn't work into anything my father wanted me to report on.

Or… maybe not. If he was here at this party, that was interesting in itself. This party was in a seedier part of town that no respectable member of the faculty would want to be seen in. Murders and rapes happened out here.

That added to the allure of him. He wasn't acting like a stuffy, boring professor. Seeing him at *this* party lent a bad-boy aura to him. He became more mysterious being here, using profanity, and complaining about me as he tasted the hard liquor.

What is wrong with you? That follow-up question hit me before he could speak. He didn't belong at this scene. He shouldn't have even known about this party.

"I didn't say anything was wrong with you, Ms. Petrov," he replied. "Just that I have this uncanny consistency of seeing you everywhere."

"Likewise," I bit out wryly. "And don't call me that."

"Ms. Petrov?" He arched one brow as he sipped his drink. "That is your name."

"A formal name, Professor." I lifted my finger from the neck of my beer bottle to gesture at the party. "And this isn't a formal setting."

"Then what should I call you?"

Oh, God. The filthy ideas that ran through my head weren't right. It wasn't right of me to lust for him, either.

"You—"

"Cops. Let's go," someone called out suddenly. The music was cut. "Cops are coming."

I glanced up at Professor Remi at the blurted-out interruption. This wouldn't only be an interruption, but also a complete halt to the evening.

"Get outta here," someone else called out.

"Move it."

"Dude, I'm leaving. Let's go."

The chaos of everyone rushing to exit rose to a confusing clamor of too much noise. Despite the fact that we had just been standing together and speaking to each other, Professor Remi and I split up, going opposite ways and getting separated in the crowd as people hurried to leave the party before the cops could come and arrest people for the drugs.

Obviously, I had to go too. I couldn't be caught by any cops, and if that became an actual threat, the guards posted outside this place would get me out.

Just as I expected, they were on high alert with the exodus of people rushing out of the party. By the time I got out, they ushered me into a car and drove me away.

"What happened?" one asked.

I shrugged, still off-kilter from talking to my professor in the unlikeliest place. "Someone called the cops, and everyone was rushing out before they were caught."

That wasn't all that happened. I'd had a strange but not bad conversation with the man I couldn't stop thinking about. And it seemed he was experiencing the same affliction.

As the car sped me away, I wished our exchange could have lasted a little longer—even if the time I spent in his intoxicating presence made me feel less sure about how to interpret his being here. At that party. On campus. In the lecture hall. Regardless of where I saw the insufferable professor who seemed to entertain a simmering resentment and suspicion of me, one thing was clear.

He wasn't going anywhere anytime soon.

And I cringed at how much that thought excited me.

7

VIKTOR

The first two weeks of pretending to be a professor hadn't gotten me anywhere with Irina. I saw her at class, where she continued to look like a bored diva. All of my students looked bored. I made the classes dull on purpose, all the better to watch them. When people were uninterested and had idle minds, they tended to let their thoughts show. Moods—other than boredom—were easier to pick up on. Maybe they let their minds wander to thoughts of things they were excited about. Or perhaps they scowled as they analyzed something they wanted to change or disliked.

Not Irina.

After two weeks, I was certain she was hiding something. I doubted it was anything like a confidential matter that the Boss could really benefit from. But I knew for a fact that she was an expert at hiding her emotions. That cool, blank ice princess mask wasn't something anyone was born with. She'd developed it. Given how young she was, I was even more intrigued why she had grown up knowing how to hide herself and look indifferent to the world.

Checking in with Lev and Rurik would hopefully give me some insight for what I was supposed to be looking for. Because so far, I had nothing. Rurik had given me a rundown when I started, but I felt like I was missing something else.

"Why am I following her again?" I asked them both after they met me for coffee the day after I saw Irina at that party.

"You're not supposed to be following her," Lev said, furrowing his brow.

"He's not," Rurik said. "He's around, but he's not actively stalking her."

I nodded. "Because this isn't my first rodeo at this shit." Smiling smugly, I let them laugh. "I'm not 'following' her, but I am making a point of running into her." It wasn't hard. The campus was large, but if I went to the commonly frequented places that staff and students visited, the odds were high that I'd cross paths with Irina without even trying to.

"You couldn't look like you're stalking her with the legions of fans interfering," Rurik teased with a shit-eating grin.

"Ah." Lev smirked. "Garnering attention, are you?"

I rolled my eyes. "It's not that bad."

Rurik laughed. "Remember the beginning of *Indiana Jones*? When he's teaching and all the students are staring at him like he hung the moon?"

I shoved at his shoulder. "I said it's not that bad."

"If only those girls knew what they were lusting for," Lev taunted. "A big, bad brothel boss."

"Nice alliteration you got there." I lifted my coffee to him, mocking him.

"Funny." He flipped me off.

Hell, I was lecturing about the English language. Crap like *alliteration* was on my mind. "They're just typical horny girls. Eager to have the whole college experience and experiment sexually." I shrugged. "I'm happy that I'm not getting the attention from anyone else on campus." And I'd noticed a few faces.

"You saw them too?" Rurik asked. He turned to Lev. "A few more Petrovs have shown up on campus."

I hadn't talked to Rurik recently either, so it was good to hear that I wasn't alone in this observation.

"More than anyone who'd be there to watch over Irina?" Lev asked.

Rurik shook his head. "They're still staying back from her. Like they were when you were on campus as Eva's bodyguard."

"They're there," I said, backing him up. "But they gave her space. I've been curious about that."

"Why?" Lev asked.

"Well, are they slacking to let her go off on her own this much? She was at that party by herself while the guards waited outside." *Or do they trust her to be able to handle herself if she gets in a bad situation?*

"They were like that when I was guarding over Eva," Lev said. "Keeping a distance."

Telling Lev about the increase of more men on campus, both from the Petrov and Ilyin families, was done now. That task was only part of what I wanted to share in this meeting. I was most interested in getting more clues about what *I* had to do.

"So, again, why am I supposed to be following Irina or getting closer to get intel from her?" I shrugged. "What exactly do you think that she could know? As far as I can tell, she's just a stuck-up brat who seems bored about going to college. Social, but never seeming close to anyone specifically."

Rurik looked at Lev, who frowned and wore a pensive expression. "We suspect she has to know something about what Igor Petrov is up to."

"Why? Just because she's his daughter?" I huffed and set my coffee mug down. "That doesn't mean shit. Oleg doesn't tell Eva everything." It was just a fact of our lives. Mafia women weren't privy to details that the men found and collected. Women simply didn't matter in terms of power—until they could serve as a pawn in an arranged marriage or breed babies for the next generation.

"Eva wouldn't be a spy," Lev argued instantly. "Oleg values her happiness too much to ever ask that of her."

I held my hand up to ward off any anger he might feel toward me for making that comparison. He was so damn protective of her. "Yes. I agree. But would Igor Petrov really rely on using his daughter as a spy? He's got plenty of men to use for that."

Rurik shrugged. "Not necessarily. Irina could be a spy and get closer to people on campus because no one would suspect her."

"That's not true. *I* suspect she's up to something. But I can't tell what."

"How does she act suspiciously around you?" Rurik asked.

"Just little things I picked up on." Nothing I could pinpoint accurately, but small quirks I noticed. She had the inner workings of a spy. She people watched, even when she tried to make it less obvious. She always sat with her back to the wall and had a vantage point that would allow her to see everything happening in a room. She had that quiet, perceptive nature, slow to engage or participate until she got a good feeling for the room or group. That wasn't a paranoid kind of behavior, but rather, soldier-like behavior.

"I wouldn't discount the idea of her being a spy," Lev warned. "Even though it would make more sense to have a soldier carry out the task of spying on anything Petrov is plotting, women have been used for surveillance. Think about some of the women you've caught at the whorehouses, wired or recording clients."

I nodded in reluctant agreement. That had happened, but it was usually a matter of a greedy and overzealous whore trying to get ahead for herself, not acting as an agent for a crime family.

"I heard some of the rumors about what the Boss sent you to Moscow to look into," Lev added. "The rumors that Sonya could have been used as a spy when she disappeared."

Again, he was right. The theory that Sonya hadn't run away with her mother floated out there, and it came with the detail that Sonya had been expected to be a spy outside of and perhaps against the Baranov organization.

"But she was so young when she disappeared." That happened years ago. "Per the lack of answers and clues I found over there, I'm more inclined to think Sonya and her mother are dead."

Neither of them replied, not agreeing or arguing with me on that point.

"Irina has to be defiant against whatever Igor is plotting or trying to do," Lev reasoned.

"Because she helped Eva escape and save you?" They had told me about that already. "That does make it sound like she would be a friend, not a foe."

"She saved Eva. If it weren't for Irina stepping up and helping her, I don't know how that day would've turned out," Lev said. "Above all else, I owe her *my* thanks for helping Eva, whatever her motivations were."

"But what would her ulterior motive be?" Rurik asked, like he was wondering aloud. "From what I saw of Eva's semester there, she and Irina didn't befriend each other. For a while, we were operating under the assumption that Irina was behind the rumors that spread about

Eva, that Eva was the reason more drugs were showing up on campus."

Lev nodded. "True."

"She had to have an ulterior motive to help Eva escape, though," I said. "And one way or another, I'll find a way to get close to her and get her to open up to me." I looked them in the eye, one at a time, serious. "I'll get her to spill her secrets to me."

"I'm surprised a ladies' man like you hasn't already," Lev teased.

Rurik grinned. "Yeah. What's taking so long?"

"I haven't gotten close to her yet." I shrugged.

"*Yet*? You're assuming you can?" Lev asked, brows raised.

They were having way too much fun with this, poking fun at me.

"She seems a bit standoffish," I admitted. Too cool and collected. Hiding her thoughts too damn well.

"If *you* can't get a woman to talk…" Rurik shook his head. "There's no hope."

"At the brothel, sure. In a club, yes." I was a dominant in those cases. "But at a college campus where I'm supposed to be her professor to get in and spy?"

Lev shrugged. "I doubt where you get her to open up matters."

"But if you're implying I could use my, um, former skills to manipulate her…"

"To seduce her?" Rurik guessed.

He and Lev both nodded.

"I'm surprised you haven't tried that already," Lev admitted.

From the first sight of her, the thought had entered my mind. I'd spent the last two weeks talking myself out of directly confronting her and trying to seduce her. My excuse for this delay was wanting to get a feeling for what I was working against. To observe, then act. But like Rurik and Lev were explaining, it wasn't clear what I was facing. It wasn't obvious what secret Irina was hiding.

"Getting too old?" Rurik teased.

"And losing your touch?" Lev joked.

I shook my head, running my hand down the stubble I needed to shave before I really had a beard again. "No. Fuckers. I'm not getting too old." I *was* older than Irina, but unlike her childish and immature peers and classmates, she posed a challenge with the difference in our ages. A thrill—to tame her, to discipline her. "I'm not losing my touch."

It would be fun to seduce my student. I had options for how I could get her to talk. Torture, bribes, ultimatums, and threats. Those were all fine techniques.

But seducing her?

It's worth a shot.

8

IRINA

Sunday night, I was driven back to my father's place for a weekly check-in. I kept a blank face on the drive there, dreading every pending second of it. To avoid falling into a completely bitter mood, I tried to concentrate on thoughts of Professor Remi.

Revisiting his dark stare at the party filled me with intrigue, chasing away the annoyance about having to speak to my father. Thinking back to how hot and hard his body was so close to mine allowed me to imagine what it could be like if he touched me, preventing me from spiraling into the irritation of facing my father.

The man was an enigma, and I relished having something independent from the usual Mafia business bullshit to focus on. He could be my secret interest, the slight source of something good instead of all the sourness and badness of my life.

But all too soon, I was in his house, looking at his smug face and dealing with the tension of not giving him the answers he wanted to hear. I couldn't give him any answers because there was nothing to report.

"You mean to tell me that you have nothing new? Nothing at all?" He held his hands up as though to say *what the fuck?* or mock me.

"Correct. I have nothing to report." I added a shrug to further convince him.

"You don't want to tell me about the increase of Ilyin men on campus?" He hardened his expression into a glare.

I shrugged again, this time, out of honest ignorance. "What's there to say? Ilyin men have always been on campus."

"What's there to say?" he snarled. "That they are there!"

I blinked, trying to rein in the sarcasm I wanted to reply with. Since he implanted me as a student at the college, Ilyin men had been present. "They've always been there."

"You don't think you need to tell me that more are there?"

For fuck's sake. "You've never asked me to count them."

"Don't get sassy with me, you little bitch."

"I'm not." Yet, I had to watch it. I was simply being honest. He could perceive this as he saw fit, though, and if he thought I was being snappy with him, he'd react by punishing Maxim to keep me in line. "I've never counted the Ilyin men. I didn't know you would want a count. Yes, I've noticed a few more of them, but not so many that it would indicate anything significant."

"What would you know about that? How the hell would you be able to determine what's significant or not?" He laughed once, smirking. "You don't know anything."

While his criticism of me was just one more way he could be sexist and cruel, I had to bite my lip.

If you think I'm so stupid and naïve, why ask me *to be your damn spy?*

"It has to be significant. If the Ilyins are trying to increase their numbers around or on campus, they are probably trying to take over the area. They must be thwarting my efforts to rule there."

I didn't reply, knowing that anything I could say would only make him madder. I didn't follow the Ilyins. I was only ever asked who was doing what. It didn't matter how many Ilyins were there. They were only there to buy or sell drugs and kind of look around, scoping out the scene.

"It's bad enough that your guards had to tell me." He narrowed his eyes and considered me like I was wasted space. "You should be upfront with me and tell me everything of interest."

Until I was a mind reader, I wouldn't be able to know what he wanted reported.

"What about the activity near the dean's office?" he asked.

I shook my head, not even having to try to look clueless. I *was* clueless. "The dean's office?"

"Yes. Keep up, you stupid bitch." He smacked his fist on the armrest of his chair. "The dean's office."

"I have nothing to do with the dean. I never go there or have to visit those offices."

"Well, you should." He grimaced as if I were the worst disappointment he could ever face. "I've heard—from your guards—that the dean has ties with a couple of up-and-coming politicians who've been on my radar."

"Okay."

"Okay? That's all you can think to say?" Shaking his head, he took a moment to collect himself. "If you can manage a simple task, you need to keep that in mind. Owen Nolan, the dean. I expect you to keep your eyes open around him."

"I've never seen him."

"So what? Snoop around his office and watch for anything you can learn about his connections with Marcus James and Eric Benson. Do I make myself clear?"

Great. Now I need to try to spy on a couple of politicians? And the dean? I nodded. "Yes."

Even though I left shortly after his order, the gloom and funkiness that came from speaking with him followed me late into the night. I was on edge, annoyed, and feeling so stuck in my life that I gave up on reading or studying in my apartment and went to the library.

Whenever I came here, I tried to snag one of the "good" spots. Up on the second floor, near the corner. So many tall bookcases stood in here that it felt like an impenetrable maze. Unfortunately, those "good" tables were all in use, despite the late hour.

I was forced to sit at a more open table near the center. As soon as I shed my coat and got my books out, I found that I couldn't concentrate here, either. The burn of someone's attention on me bothered me. Someone was watching me.

One look around provided the source. Andre Ilyin, one of the familiar faces among my father's rivals, stared at me from a table on the opposite side of the room. Without a book, notepad, tablet, or laptop on the table in front of him, he stood out. He looked out of place, a lone man dressed in all black, just staring at me.

Andre wasn't merely looking. He was checking me out, smiling wickedly as though he could use X-ray vision and see what I wore beneath my sweater and jeans.

It didn't make me feel good. Having his too-hungry gaze on me left me feeling soiled and damaged. Like he wasn't only staring at me but touching me, and that wasn't a caress I wanted to experience. Ever.

Sighing heavily, I tried to ignore him, not even glancing in his direction. It wouldn't be the first time a Mafia man—even a rival—had given me once-overs like that. At parties, balls, and galas. At dinners and holiday events. I'd been around them before, and I'd learned to just accept that they would look all they wanted. Treating women respectfully wasn't something that happened in this world. We were to be used and owned, nothing more.

Until I can leave. Until I can kill him and disappear...

The pep talk that I'd only need to put up with Mafia men until I ended my father's life didn't prompt me to feel much better, though.

What did was spotting Professor Remi in the corner.

He was there, reading or pretending to. And it was *his* stare on me that distracted me from the life that I didn't want. Having his smoldering gaze on me lit me up. Letting him check me out gave me a sense of worth. It tricked me into assuming he would value me. He would want me—and it would just be *me*. Professor Remi was just a man, a hot one, one I shouldn't want, but he was not affiliated with the Mafia, as far as I knew. If he was associated with any Family, the guards would report about it and tell my father.

I smiled, tracing the tip of my pen along my closed lips, reveling in how good it made me feel that a sexy man could see me as a woman, not as Igor's daughter.

That good feeling stayed with me all night and into the morning. On the walk to his lecture in the morning, I breathed in deeply, letting my lungs fill with the crisp morning air.

I felt more alive. I was more excited for the day, not worrying about how slowly it would drag. The excitement and anticipation of being able to see Professor Remi—especially after witnessing his interest in me last night at the library—had that much of a difference on my mood.

Arriving early in the hopes of getting a good seat up in the front, I strode into the hall and sipped my coffee, an essential for every morning here. Taking a longer walk, since I had the time, I headed down the corridor that would bring me past his office. I had no reason to go there. I doubted I ever would. No professors saw me in their offices because I was—on paper—an excellent student who never needed tutoring or extra help. Even though I was at college as a role to fulfill for my father, I was a good student with little assistance to maintain good grades.

Still, I knew where Professor Remi's office was. I neared it now, slowing down in case I could treat myself to an extra eyeful of him. When I reached his open door, though, the vision that greeted me wasn't one I wanted to savor.

A tall redhead leaned in toward him, angling her head up and closing her eyes in preparation of bringing her face close to his. Just as I set my foot down in the hallway, the heel of my boot clicked loudly because I was so surprised.

Whoever this woman was, dressed in an office-chic pantsuit with the lowest cut possible, she had every intention of kissing the professor I couldn't stop myself from desiring.

As she slanted toward him, likely trying to capitalize on the element of surprise, Professor Remi shifted his head a little to dodge her reaching him.

"Oh." I let that interjection pop out of my mouth like I meant to say *whoops*. "My bad. I didn't realize this was a private moment."

The woman straightened before she could fall from Professor Remi's evading her. As she faced me, with him holding her back at arm's length, she shot me a beady glare that suggested she wished I'd drop dead or buzz off.

I'd interrupted their moment. She was pissed. But as my professor met my gaze, I couldn't tell whether he was annoyed or grateful. It wasn't clear if he begrudged me for interrupting or if he was irked with this woman for making a move on him like that. He didn't look happy, that was for sure. But was he bothered by me or her?

"Just passing by on my way to class," I said, already moving my feet to walk away.

Once I did, I scolded myself for the flicker of jealousy that burned in me.

Jealous? What right did I have to be jealous?

Professor Remi was just my teacher.

A crush on my professor was quite possibly the stupidest thing I could fill my head with. It was such a silly concern, a non-issue in the big picture of what was happening in my life.

I don't have time for this. He could kiss whoever he wanted, and any woman could try her best with him. It didn't matter to me. It couldn't matter to me.

Romance was dead to me. It had to be because I'd never have the freedom to actually decide something *I* wanted. I'd never have the right to act on something that interested me.

The intel of Professor Remi kissing some assistant in the building wouldn't make Igor Petrov happy. And failing to appease my father with the information he did want wouldn't help Maxim.

Still, as I entered the lecture room, I pushed the doors too hard. Anger simmered in my veins. My head wasn't cleared of the annoyance and frustration. My heart raced, and no matter how many times I mentally scolded myself to snap out of this and forget about having a secret crush on my professor, I couldn't force the strong feelings away.

Settling in for the lecture to start, I fought hard to find that stupid, trivial optimism I'd woken with.

But it was gone.

9

VIKTOR

I told you no.

Jessica hadn't stopped coming on to me since the day we met. It didn't matter what the message was. She always had a reason to stop by my office.

Today, it was to confirm that I would pick up another class for a few weeks. Another faculty member had been in a car accident and would be off for a month. Since I was only teaching the one class that Irina was in, I had free time. I didn't want to get tied up with another course since I wasn't actually here to work for long, only as long as my cover required it. However, the other class, a poetry one, was short. And Irina was enrolled in it. An additional chance to see her would be productive.

I didn't need Jessica to personally tell me that picking up this class was confirmed. I'd already spoken with the head of the department. The dean's office wouldn't be involved in this kind of an arrangement, so she had no hand in this to come speak to me about it at all. But I wasn't born yesterday. I was aware of her eagerness to see me, no matter what. Perhaps she was one of those thrill junkies, always going for what she couldn't have. My rejection could very well be the motivation for her to try harder.

Even going as far as leaning in to kiss me.

Irina had been walking by right then, and the timing of her heels loudly clacking on the floor was kismet. I was so glad that she'd interrupted.

"Don't try that again," I warned Jessica as I backed up to pick up my laptop bag. My lecture would begin in a couple of minutes.

"You know you want me." She grinned, sitting on the edge of my desk.

I grabbed a file that she sat on, and I used enough force that it made her jerk to the side and stand again. Pouting for real, she furrowed her brow at me like she couldn't believe I'd done that.

"I don't." I pointed the file at her as I rounded the desk. "Don't assume you ever know a single thing about me."

She hugged herself, still smiling. "I like it, this air of mystery you keep around yourself."

I was no mystery, just careful about who I dealt with and what they could know about my real life—the version of me that included the Mafia.

"Don't bother me again." I left with that warning, not even caring that she remained in my office. Nothing incriminating was in there. I hardly touched anything, and I never wrote down anything that someone could trace back to me. Most of the paperwork had become obsolete, anyway. Documentation was all done via emails and online for courses and the registration of job positions.

Leaving her behind me might have given her the wrong idea, but there wasn't anything I could do to change her idea that my office was always open to her. There would be no stopping her, not when she used her relationship to the dean as a means of demanding clout.

I hurried to the lecture, anxious and impatient to get there. Seeing Irina was a priority. I had to assess how she was reacting to catching me almost kissing another woman. If I were going to adopt the method of seducing her to get her to open up and talk to me about what Igor Petrov was up to, I couldn't look "taken" and with another woman.

Irina was seated in the middle of the auditorium seating, and she didn't react to my entrance. Most students shut up, used to my stern and strict protocol of beginning as soon as I walked into the room. I would often start with another mind-numbing lecture as I approached the podium, but I didn't today. With the quiet hanging over the room, all eyes on me—except for Irina's—it was hard not to feel like I had such a grand entrance. Like I was royalty sweeping into court.

"Morning. Let's begin," I said firmly as I reached my spot behind the podium. Plugging in my laptop took seconds, and connecting my slides to the overhead screen took even less time than that. Everything went as seamlessly as ever, and I spoke as I got set up.

This lecture was as dry as the rest of them, but I didn't yawn this time. All the while I talked, I noticed Irina.

She was upset. I didn't need any more background or any more time to learn her tells. I knew she was upset.

Glum, looking down, seeming entirely uninterested. She had checked out of anything to do with this class.

If she's only here to be a spy for Igor, then that would make sense. She wouldn't put much effort forward if she only had to be on campus to get intel for her father.

I would've been convinced that theory had to be true if she didn't have great grades in the class so far. In the poetry class I had just picked up, she had lower scores, but that didn't indicate anything. Poetry was... lame.

No matter how many times I tried to call on Irina to get her to answer questions, I couldn't get a rise out of her. This woman was just a shell now, a numbed, vacant-eyed person who was apathetic to the entire first half of the class. I couldn't get her to react to my stern instructions or difficult questions. If anyone else in the class commented about it, they'd be correct in saying I was singling her out and picking on her.

What the hell?

I was obsessed with getting a reaction out of her. I wanted to see that defensive, sassy spark that I witnessed when we ran into each other at that party off campus. I wanted to see her pupils dilate with interest when I stepped into her personal space. I wished to hear her hitched breath when I cursed and drank like I was just an ordinary, hard man, not a polished professor with manners and polite actions.

As I neared the halfway point of the lecture, when I would switch over to giving a pop quiz, a thought hit me, and I couldn't shake it off.

Is she... jealous? I couldn't help but wonder if she was acting so moody and glum like this because she saw another woman with me.

The second I tried to dismiss that, I had to fight to keep a smile from breaking over my face.

Jealous.

If she could envy Jessica leaning in for a kiss, that was proof that she wanted me herself. If she could stoop to being jealous, that was evidence of her caring. Of her wanting me.

And I liked it.

The pop quizzes didn't take long, all administered online since everyone had a tablet or laptop with them. Grades came in immediately, scored with the program I used because I sure as hell wasn't grading shit manually.

Before I could log in to see how Irina scored, I could guess that she'd blown it. She'd answered too quickly, barely seeming to take enough time to read through the questions.

"Ms. Petrov," I called out as she gathered her bag and coat to leave. A small thread of excitement lit up inside me at calling her by her name.

"Then what should I call you?"

I'd asked her that when she insisted I not use her name at the party. Her claim that it wasn't a formal situation that would require a formal name didn't fly with me. When she said that, though, I got hung up on the thought of being in an even more informal setting with her. An indecent one, too.

She stiffened at my calling out her name. Slowly, she faced me, glaring with such a haughty yet defensive glower that I was turned on instantly.

Facing off with a fierce woman was always a pleasure. Because I would always tame them. The ride to getting them to submit was one of my favorite experiences.

She arched one brow, waiting. The fact that she wouldn't speak but rely on nonverbal communication went to show how aloof she could be.

Be a challenge, sweetheart. See what happens. I dare you.

"Please wait after class to speak with me," I said. While I made sure to come off as polite, I left no room for her to interpret that as anything but an order.

She dipped her chin slightly, almost in a nod, and that was all the response she'd give me.

The wait for the rest of the students to file out of the room felt like an eternity of anticipation. Every moment that passed felt longer than the ones before. By the time that it took for everyone to leave, I was damn near bursting with desire and adrenaline. The whole while,

Irina sat in the front row, one leg crossed over the other, her foot bobbing almost as a fidget of tapping it on the floor. Her arms remained crossed, which only pushed the swells of her breasts up higher, emphasizing them even though she wore a turtleneck sweater and no flesh was bared. Her long, brown hair tumbled over her shoulders as she waited for me to address her. But it was the cool expression of waiting on her face that showed her ire with me.

Her guards remained in the hall. I knew it for a fact because I'd seen them pass by then duck their heads in throughout the class. They could wait.

I doubted I'd have long to speak with her without the Petrov guards getting suspicious, but they didn't know me. Because I wasn't often in the field, they wouldn't know me as Viktor Baranov but as Professor Remi, who would have every right to speak to one of his students after class.

The doors closed after the last person exited, and sure enough, one of the Petrov thugs peered through the glass, seeing Irina seated in the front row and me at the podium. Once the man passed by, shrugging, I approached her.

It was just me and her. At last. We'd shared a private moment of just talking at that party, but it was far too brief of an interaction. This time, I could control what happened.

"It's obvious that you're going to need some help."

She huffed, giving me a look of contempt. "Oh."

That attitude. Oh, I was really liking the idea of spanking it right out of her. Fucking it out of her.

"If you're not aware yet, I'll be taking over the poetry course Mr. Gannon was teaching."

She lifted one shoulder and let it fall in a half-ass shrug as she stood. "I am aware. The email came through during your lecture—as scintillating yet bone-dry as ever."

I smiled, amped up with the thrill of her trying to goad me or taunt me.

Bring it on, sweetheart. Try me.

"And you're also blowing through the quizzes in this course."

Letting her coat hang over her bag, she dropped her arm as she shrugged again.

Her indifference was confusing, and it intrigued me. She was clearly smart. I saw the evidence of that fact in the scores from the things she actually applied herself to. It seemed she harbored some kind of a laziness, though, not caring at times but then willing to do her work at others.

"College is a waste of my time," she admitted.

Because you're only here to spy for your father? To act as an agent for him?

"Fine. But I warn you not to waste *my* time." I leaned over the desk at the front, staring at her intensely. "Or else."

She blinked once, showing that I'd cracked her. It was the barest and slightest reaction, but I saw it.

"*Or else?*" she parroted, disbelief in her breathy tone.

Desire swirled in the depths of her blue eyes, and I had to remind myself not to growl. To lunge for her. To act on this attraction that simmered between us like a live wire.

"Yeah." I tipped my chin up higher, relishing the idea of being able to carry out that promise of *or else*. She could benefit from discipline, but she'd absolutely soar from pleasure if I treated her to my idea of discipline.

"Or. Else," I repeated.

10

IRINA

Or else?

Damn him.

Damn this cocky bastard.

My professor had no business issuing a threat like that. If any man could get away with telling me *or else*, it'd be my father. And he only had that power over me because he'd demonstrated time and time again that he could do whatever the hell he wanted to my younger brother and it would be insurance against my ever disobeying.

But Professor Remi? How the hell did he think he could punish me for wasting his time?

I *wasn't* wasting his time. If I wanted to blow off my classes, that was my prerogative. No one else's. He couldn't care. He didn't have any stakes in my grades. I was—for all he could assume—one student among hundreds that he'd grade and decide to pass or fail.

I refused to entertain the idea that he could care. He didn't know me to care, but then again, no one ever really knew *me*.

"And just what does that mean?" I asked, playing with fire and loving the giddiness that came with it. This was like poking the bear. Like skating on thin ice. Dangerous, but so damn exciting that I couldn't pass up on the opportunity.

"What do you think it means, Irina?"

Oh, he was playing dirty now. "Irina?"

He nodded, slowly walking around the desk to approach me from where I stood on the opposite side of it. "Yes, Irina."

I fought the instinct to shiver. Hearing my name rolling off his tongue like that felt like a caress. Like a tender touch or summons. He was just so serious, so gruff and hard despite this image of a professional and by-the-books professor he had perfected.

"Do you call all your students by their first names? I thought you were all about formality."

"That's what I'm calling you. For now." He continued to stalk closer to me, his deep brown stare boring into me and making me more turned on than I'd ever been. Having this tall, sexy man stalk toward me had me reeling from the sensation of being prey. Hunted prey.

Do you refer to all your other students with that deep, rich bedroom voice, too?

I hoped he didn't. I wanted to feel special, to feel seen by him.

"For now?" I asked.

He nodded, stepping right up into my personal space, just like he had done at that party last week. Immediately, his body heat and scent hit me, and I hated how badly I wanted to lean into his touch, to fall into his arms and let him catch me and hold me.

Looking down at me, he forced me to crane my neck to peer up at his serious and intense gaze. This man wasn't just challenging me not to look away. He was giving me a preview of what it felt like when a man was wholly focused on a woman.

"Yeah. For now," he replied, lowering his voice even more.

"What else would you call me?" I asked. The second the words left my mouth, I shuddered under the drugging charge of carrying on with this conversation I had no business having with my professor. With any man.

He was flirting with me. Hitting on me. It was such a novel experience, something that hadn't even happened with someone outside of the Mafia world, that I didn't want it to ever stop.

"I would call you whatever I wanted," he said, like a rich promise of sinister intent. "It doesn't matter what I'd call you. If you think you can get away with wasting my time, I'll punish you."

Oh.

My.

God.

I swallowed hard. My mouth was suddenly so dry as my heart raced too fast. I couldn't fill my lungs with enough air, dizzy with this haze of tension that claimed me. I had no experience with talking to a man like this. I had zero background in handling these kinds of sexy scenarios to rely on for guidance.

The idea of him punishing *me*, showing me how he'd want me to behave, was such a naughty thought I could barely stand it. Already sucking in a gasp, I sounded like a wanton woman, held on the edge of a line that bordered logic and desire.

I wasn't a fan of pain, but with one long study of my professor's wicked stare on me, I just knew that his brand of pain wouldn't be something I'd dread but something I'd yearn for. His idea of pain would somehow bring me so much pleasure.

"You think you could punish me?" I retorted when I could speak after the shock settled in my mind.

"I don't *think* I could, Irina." He stepped forward again, brushing his leg against mine.

I didn't think it was possible for him to be any closer. I didn't realize how potent the faintest touch against him could unravel my resolve to look unaffected and stay strong.

"I *will*," he promised instead. "If you want to push your luck with me, if you want to try me..." He laughed once, a low chuckle that reinforced his deep, gruff voice. "Fuck around and find out."

I slid the tip of my tongue along my lower lip, needing moisture there from my jaw dropping and breathing so quickly and shallowly for him. I'd never been so turned on in my life, but seeing his gaze darken as he tracked the movement of my tongue aroused me even more. Witnessing how *I* impacted him was a heady triumph to enjoy.

"How dare you talk to me like this, Professor Remi—"

He grabbed my hand, clutching it not gently but not cruelly either. "Viktor," he corrected. "You will call me Viktor."

"Because you're tossing out all formality, telling me to fuck around and push you?"

His responding grin was so slow and sexy that I wished I could have the courage to kiss it right off his face.

"Because I want to hear you say my name, Irina. I want to see how your face lights up when you say it."

"Lighting up with anger, maybe," I argued.

"Or desire." He began to thread his fingers between mine. The reminder that he still held my hand—a privilege he'd helped himself to without asking me—prompted me to wrench it away. Yanking my hand back, I resisted the sensation of missing his touch.

"You've got no clue what you're messing with," I told him. I wanted to say it matter-of-factly, but I sounded too breathy and turned on to come off as a serious woman right now.

"You've got no clue *who* you're messing with," I added.

In the back of my mind, though, I knew I was just bluffing. I wasn't really protected. I had no backup to save me if Viktor actually intended to punish me for wasting his time or being disobedient.

I might have had guards assigned to me my whole life, but that was nothing more than a standard Igor Petrov extended to protect his assets. I was a spy, the only female member of the family who'd stand in for an operation. Because of that, Igor had confidently categorized me as an expendable, replaceable pawn.

Past that duty to be loyal and do as my father ordered, no one cared about me. No one would actually care about what happened to me—so long as I always did what I was told. Not a single person in the entire Petrov Family would wonder what happened to me. The guards out in the hall might worry for a moment because they'd look like they were slacking on the clock if something happened to me.

Beyond them, not a single soul would care if I was harmed. Or if I was manipulated and treated poorly. If I was subjected to whatever Viktor envisioned for my so-called punishment,

My younger brother would care. He was always the only one who would hope I was safe and all right. Maxim was all I had, but if something awful happened to me, I wouldn't want him to have to suffer the gruesome facts of my being punished.

I lowered my gaze, swept away by this current of depression. The sobering thought that no one could care about me took me really low. I didn't often let myself feel depressed, as if one could have that depth of control over me and my actions. Preferring to channel my negative thoughts and energy into anger was much better.

Forget it.

Just forget it, Irina.

Turning away from Viktor, I fought the longing to be facing him again. Over my shoulder, I tossed back one last insult. "This conversation is a waste of my time."

I didn't have a chance to slip away or leave with the last word. He lunged forward, shooting his hand at me until he grabbed hold of my wrist. He didn't only reach out and snag my wrist, though. He pulled me back and spun me until my back slammed into the wall of a small alcove near the podium.

I let out a shocked exhale, the air punched out of me at his rough handling. He would be in so much trouble if word got out that he'd put his hands on me at all. Caged in, with my back against the cold wall, I held my breath with the certainty that he was leaning in to kiss me. Now, after every one of my twenty-three years, I could tip my chin up and prepare to be kissed. For the first time.

I'd never been kissed, never allowed to get close to a man to want to kiss him or let him kiss me.

"I mean it, Irina. Try me. Test me."

I wanted to, so badly.

"Be a naughty girl for me and see what happens."

It was too enticing to be given a free ticket to push this strong, sexy man. It was a once-in-a-lifetime opportunity, and I dove in to take advantage. He couldn't have any idea what his words were doing to me. I was melting, so turned on I could barely think straight. My nipples beaded under my sweater and bra. My panties clung to me, stickier with my arousal on the fabric.

"Try me and see what happens." He paired those serious yet taunting words at me with another inch lost between us. He slanted toward me, intent on getting intimate and being so bold as to kiss me.

I lowered my lids, wanting to close my eyes just to fully savor the touch of his mouth on mine.

But it didn't happen. Our sexy, flirty moment stopped the second my phone buzzed. This tone indicated a phone call coming in from one of the two people who ever did call me—Maxim as video calls so he could read my lips and use sign language when he was permitted use of his guard's phone, and my father.

The screen showed nothing that I'd recognize, but this call had to matter. It seemed similar to the number for the old guard who supervised my younger brother.

"Hello?" I stepped back from Viktor, needing space away from him to just think.

The call ended, but a text message popped up just as quickly.

Attacks are happening near the building. Do not approach until the scene is clear.

Near Maxim's building.

The guard must have sent it to me and my usual driver. Anyone being attacked near the filthy building Maxim lived in would always be terrible news. Awful news that I couldn't do anything about.

Please, please be safe. I wasn't sure how I'd move on if I lost Maxim or he was hurt. Again, I hated that he had to be a prisoner in that specific building, in that lousy part of town. Being reminded of the situation doused the flames of attraction and desire that had been growing here with Viktor.

"I…" I backpedaled from Viktor, not letting his expression of surprise and confusion get to me. I couldn't. Not now. Not ever. He wasn't supposed to be talking with a student like that. And definitely not a student like me.

"I need to go." Turning so quickly that I almost lost my balance, I ran toward the door.

LEONA WHITE

My worry about my brother trumped this stubborn interest I couldn't shake for Professor Viktor Remi.

Because if there was one thing I'd gamble on, it was that this interest would go nowhere.

11

VIKTOR

I couldn't believe that she left me like that. That she'd taken the courage to bolt.

She had been putty in my hands until her phone buzzed with a text. Whoever contacted her had given her bad news, because that was the only explanation I could think of that would have caused her to go from a flushed face of arousal, so excited about kissing me and keeping up with this flirty conversation, to a pale expression of dread. She could barely speak, rushing away, and while I didn't know everything about her, I was clued in enough that her stammering speech wasn't the norm.

If she hadn't given me a sign that she'd been wanting me back, I would've believed her sudden departure. But she had been into it, intrigued by what I said and curious about how I broke the rules to touch her.

Her quitting on that pissed me off. I wasn't so far into the act that I couldn't have reined myself in. I was in control, and of course, sometimes, things don't go as planned. That was life. In the art and game of seduction, I had to be ready for anything ranging from rejection to eagerness.

"She wasn't debating it," I reminded myself as I walked across campus to check in with Rurik. All night and all morning, I obsessed about why she'd taken off and what I could do next. Rurik's call to check in with me was a slight distraction, but still, Irina was at the forefront of my mind.

There was no way in hell I was abandoning my plan to seduce her. When I first told the other two that I'd try to get closer to Irina and get her to open up that way, I intended to use that method as just part of the job that I had to do to get answers.

After I saw the fire in her eyes, it was hard not to get addicted. Likewise, when that fire and interest dimmed, I was greedy and impatient in wanting to know what happened to make her lose her spirit so suddenly, what thoughts she could've had to make her frown so quickly.

Maybe something to do with whatever spooked her to run away?

I would drive myself insane speculating, and I didn't intend to all day. She would be at the poetry class, so I could look forward to another chance of seeing her there. I doubted she'd mention our conversation from yesterday, but dammit, I wanted to bring it up and get a rise out of her. I wanted to complete the unfinished business of her closing her eyes and leaning in toward me, completely committed to a kiss.

Rurik was already seated at the coffee shop. This smaller vendor spot wasn't one that Irina ever went to, so I felt safe that I could concentrate on whatever Rurik had to say for at least five minutes.

"Hey," I greeted. "I don't have much time."

He nodded, gesturing at the coffee he'd already ordered for me. "I know."

"Oh." I raised my brows. "Thanks." I took a seat across from him and brought the black coffee up toward my lips. "I didn't realize you'd be bribing me to talk."

"No." He chuckled at my weak joke. "I just figured I was throwing your morning game off, asking you to meet up before you have to 'work'."

"Well, thanks." I set the cup down after a sip. "So, what's up?"

Something urgent, or else he wouldn't have texted to meet. He wasn't even here all the time, expected to carry out surveillance on a variety of projects.

"I was listening in to some of the men near the library late last night."

I laughed lightly. "When I heard that big library was open twenty-four, seven, I thought it was a joke."

He nodded. "They just changed the hours like that. I guess to better accommodate all the late-night students who wanted to use it."

"I saw." Hell, when I went to college before Oleg needed me elsewhere for the family, the library was for studying and the nights were for partying. Then again, some of the people who pretended to study there had seemed to be prepping for a line or shooting up before a party. Maybe the library had become a stop in getting ready for the usual nighttime mayhem college students got up to.

"Anyway, I was close enough to listen in to some people, and it sounds like the Ilyins who've been hanging around lately are to blame for the rapes last night."

I furrowed my brow. The concept of rape wasn't anything scandalous, not to me. After the many years I'd supervised the whorehouses for the Boss, it was something I'd dealt with a lot. Both in ensuring no clients or guests were raping women and getting away without pay, and also that the elite whores weren't being abused. Another brother managed the sex clubs. That was a whole different niche and branch of the family's revenue. Weirder, kinkier shit happened there, but the whorehouses were supposed to be more of the standard fucking. Exceptions happened, of course, but it was in our best interests to keep good talent. Better whores meant better-paying clients.

"Last night?" I asked. I knew from the background the men had given me that the increase of drugs being circulated often resulted in more rapes and attacks being reported. But hell, that shit would happen until the end of time, and not just here, but all over the world. We weren't here to try to police anything. It wasn't our business how often women were being raped. I did care, though, so I took this news in consideration of how it could affect my mission here.

Rurik nodded. "Yeah. It sounds like the Ilyin men are getting more daring in being seen, not only in pushing drugs, but looping women in for business and pleasure, if you get what I'm saying."

I shook my head, slightly unprepared for all the politics and drama that would need to be puzzled out on an assignment like this. At the whorehouses, or even those few weeks I'd spent in Moscow to follow up on those leads about Sonya, everything was cut and dry. I knew what I had to do. I could count on all the players to be who they were, and that was that.

Here, it seemed like one complicated layer popped up after another.

"I can't stand those Ilyin fuckers." The Petrovs weren't any better, but the Ilyins had always seemed so much more prone to whining that they had a bad rep.

"Me neither," Rurik said.

"And I thought I saw Andre Ilyin near the commons yesterday, too."

Again, he agreed with a nod. "I've seen him here lately as well."

Andre wasn't necessarily anyone special, but he was a determined soldier, never giving up on a hit even if his boss changed his orders after the fact.

"I just wanted to tell you in person to keep an extra careful lookout for them. When they bring in more drugs, the influx takes a while to steady out."

"You mean more reports about rapes and attacks will be coming in yet?"

"Exactly."

He left after that brief check-in, and I hurried to get to the other building, one I didn't often go to, in order to stand in for this poetry class. On the walk there, I ignored the falling snow and bite of the cold wind. I was too stuck in my head to care about the shitty weather.

What if something like that happened to Irina?

I had no claim on her. She was just a target I was supposed to follow and weed out intel from.

Yet, I hated the very thought of her being hurt or used. I could tell from her reactions yesterday that she was inexperienced, even in the moment leading up to a kiss. If Igor had done anything right, she was still a virgin, awaiting the fiancé Igor would choose for her.

Now that the thought had gotten in my head, I couldn't dislodge it. I couldn't stop worrying about something bad happening to the cool, aloof brunette who'd captured my attention as something more than a target.

How the fuck did she get under my skin like this?

I was concerned about her, already reading too far into her reaction to a text yesterday, her hot-and-cold responses to my leaning in toward her. Now, as I entered the building and hurried up to reach the smaller classroom than the lecture hall I was used to, I battled with the worry that she could end up like all the other victims.

She was a target, that wouldn't change, but as I braced myself to see her in the classroom, I had to admit to myself that she had also become so much more.

Irina represented a challenge, and I was tasked with getting her to spill some clues and answers.

However, I'd be a world-class liar if I said I wasn't too vested in making sure she was safe, too.

12

IRINA

After I left the building, rushing away from that hot moment I was sharing with Professor Remi, I sought out my guards. They kept their distance, but I was never lost from them. I could always locate them nearby.

"What's going on?" I demanded of the first man I saw. They were usually around in twos, a pair. That was a standard for security details. Never alone, a backup on call and within reach.

He shrugged. "What do you mean?"

"Where's the other?" I asked. "Peter." I seldom referred to them by name. There was never any need to because we didn't speak to each other. Part of their reasoning to stay back from me was to eliminate anyone thinking we were together so I could look approachable. Asking why this guard was alone didn't fit into this urgent need to know what was going on near my brother, but it struck me as odd so I blurted the question.

"Following up on the latest incident," he said, arching his brows as if questioning why I'd ask and make contact with him directly and also surprise that he'd answered me at all.

"The attacks near Maxim?" I shoved my hands into my coat pockets, cold and unhappy about it. Summer felt so far away with this snow falling.

He furrowed his brow. "What attacks?"

"What incident are you talking about?" I asked instead. What *else* was going on?

"The Ilyins." He glanced around, as if someone were listening in. It was just the two of us out here in the cold near the building. "They're rumored to be behind all the new drugs on campus. Spreading them and raping women."

Again? Another piece of my heart chipped off and shriveled. I *hated* that my father was instigating this drug war, that he was a perpetrator and cause of any woman being abused or raped. It was all the more reason for me to kill him, to end him and his plans. It was a small part I could do to help. In the back of my mind, I knew that someone else would step into his place and do the same thing, though.

"What are *you* talking about?" he asked.

It was ironic that the guards could double as spies here. If they could manage that job, why did my father insist on using me here?

"I received a message that attacks were happening near my brother's building."

He shrugged, still looking out for anyone approaching us. "So?"

So? I wished I could hit him and get away with it. Fury lanced through me, heating me up and making me want to scream at the injustice of it all.

"I want to make sure he's okay." He couldn't have received the same text I had been sent, not if he was clueless about it happening. That had to mean he hadn't received the text that said to stay away from that area.

"No." He narrowed his eyes. "You can't decide when you visit him. I was told you wouldn't be seeing him until the end of the month."

Dammit! There was no way I could wait that long, not with news of violence near him in that crappy part of town.

"I insist," I said coolly.

He laughed once, as if he were dealing with a pesky irritation, not a valid request. "I don't think so."

"Then take me to my father."

That wouldn't solve anything, either. He wouldn't bend and let me visit Maxim just because I asked or demanded. But maybe he'd slip and tell me what was going on.

To my surprise, the guard agreed to arrange for my driver to come and collect me. He joined the driver in the front seat, and they discussed the possibility of Ilyin men causing trouble on campus. Causing trouble was what the Mafia did. They used power and danger and violence as tokens of business, but they had to be on top of it all in this dog-eat-dog world.

On the drive to my father's, I tried not to panic and get sucked into too much worry about Maxim. The guard there would keep him safe. He wouldn't let him be harmed unnecessarily.

My father rolled his eyes at me when I arrived, almost as if he'd counted on me to show up, worried.

"I don't know why you waste your time thinking about that worthless boy."

He's my brother!

I bit my tongue and tried to remain patient. "Is he all right?"

He dismissed me with a wave. "Yes. He's alive."

Alive? That's it? "Was he hurt?"

"No. He's been temporarily relocated, and no, I'm not telling you where. He's safe there."

I crossed my arms. "You expect me to spy and snoop on those politicians while you hide him from me?"

Igor Petrov played hardball, but even he could respect when he was pushing me too hard. "He's safe where he is. Another apartment. Near the docks."

I gaped at him. "What? In those moldy apartments?" I knew just the ones he was talking about. They were disgusting, often used as torture cells for anyone they'd captured.

"It'll do for now until the Ilyins stop fighting near his usual place."

That was a clue I'd save for later. *The Ilyins are behind whatever violence is going on.* They were a number-one enemy and rival at the time. Since my father hadn't succeeded in getting to the Baranovs at all, and Lev had escaped, that Family had retreated. I still saw Rurik on campus now and then, but the Baranovs had all but retreated from the drug and turf war in and around the college area. I couldn't blame Oleg Baranov for backing out from this mess. He wasn't stupid, and he was familiar with how my father would screw over anyone and everyone to get ahead.

Something was brewing with the Ilyins. They were rumored to be behind the recent increase of drugs and rapes on campus. This danger out in the rougher part of town… What weren't they up to?

"Find him a better place," I told my father. "Maxim can't live in those conditions. Not with his risk for infections." His difficult experience at childbirth had resulted in his being weak and immunocompromised. He'd become deaf from the strong medications and treatments they'd used on him in the NICU to keep him alive.

"He'll live wherever I put him."

I bit my tongue, watching my temper. I had to negotiate, not lash out. "He deserves a life. Not to be a prisoner."

"Maybe if he weren't such a weak waste of space," my father argued, "he might."

Staring at him with all the hatred my soul could contain, I vowed it again.

I'm going to kill you. I will rid the world of your evil and I will enjoy every second of killing you.

Maxim was an innocent victim. So was I. And one day, I would right those wrongs.

"Maxim isn't a priority," he reminded me.

Not to you. But he most certainly was to me. I was the only one rooting for him.

"*Your* priority is staying on campus and doing as you're told. Find out what you can about who was raped last night. Look into James and Benson. Have something to fucking report to me for once."

I was dismissed. Like a tool, a discarded *thing*, he sent me away.

All night, I couldn't avoid worrying about my brother. This anxiety was nothing new, but the more that it gnawed on me, the worse I felt. It was a consuming, relentless beast, taking my every thought and stealing my ability to function in any other way.

If I were to lose Maxim, I would have nothing. I would have no one. He was the only source of anything good in my life, and I couldn't stomach losing him or knowing he could suffer any further.

Because of this stress, I slept terribly. Nothing helped. Not a jog on the treadmill at the apartment's gym. Not a snack. Not TV, even the lamest documentary I could find. Reading was a no-go as well, since I couldn't focus enough to actually absorb a single word of what my gaze swept over. Homework preoccupied me a little bit, but it wasn't until very late that my eyes closed and I attempted to sleep. I ended up oversleeping, setting a very lousy mood for the rest of the day.

Getting up hours late had me rushing to reach campus on time, but despite my best hurried efforts, I felt not like myself. Exhaustion nipped at me as I walked toward the building my first class was in. I didn't stop for coffee first, which was so unlike me. I needed caffeine in the morning like a plant needed water.

Knowing I'd be seeing Professor Remi should've put a little extra pep in my step and encouraged me to look forward to this class, but I was too tired and stressed to let anything cut through my mood.

I arrived late, something that I loathed with a passion. Punctuality was an elemental feature of success, no matter the situation. It was especially annoying in the classroom. My time here was a joke. I wasn't here to study for a career, but at times, it was interesting. It was fun to sometimes pretend I was here as an intellectual, living an ordinary life like all the other students who had a bright future ahead of them. My future would only begin once I killed my father, so I supposed I couldn't get far in wanting to be like everyone else outside the Mafia circles.

When a professor or instructor was late, it held the whole class back, as though our time wasn't valuable or respected. When a student arrived late, sneaking in after the lesson or class had begun, it was a frustrating distraction.

This time, I was the one sneaking in, closing the door behind me as quietly as I could.

Without the usual ample morning downtime to get myself dressed and ready today, I felt sloppier than usual, not put together like I preferred. And it showed.

I turned from closing the door, feeling everyone's eyes on me as I entered. I was in the spotlight now, and I hated it when I didn't look my best.

Worst of all, though, was the sensation of Professor Remi's eyes on me. Viktor's gaze. He paused mid-sentence at my arrival, and he stared at me with something between contempt and curiosity, a bizarre range that triggered me to feel self-conscious. With how I'd last spent time near him, I was on edge.

Had he been leaning in to kiss me?

Was his talking dirty like that a prank?

I couldn't decipher his expression as he watched me walk into the room and take a seat. He was even better at masking his emotions than I was—cool and blank-faced but with a low-lying burn of anger hinted at in his steely glare.

"Ms. Petrov," he said loudly.

Dammit. I loathed hearing my name. I couldn't stand the reminder that I was my father's daughter. But I knew better than to wish for him to call me Irina in front of the class. Hearing my name roll off his tongue was a private treat I wanted to treasure and keep to myself.

"Nice of you to join us." He lowered his gaze toward the podium, returning to what he had been reviewing. "You will come to my office this evening for the material you've missed."

Shit. I nodded, though, not in the mood to make a scene or argue. I *was* late, and I had missed a lot today. His announcement wasn't an offer or request, but an order. Regardless of how he conveyed the message, it was one more thing for me to deal with.

I was anxious about Maxim being near violence or being cooped up in low-quality housing. I was furious with my father's treatment of me and my brother, wishing I could just kill him now or run away. And now I had to deal with Viktor being on my ass about classwork.

I sighed heavily, regretting that I hadn't stopped for coffee. Being here in college was a ruse. It was a big game of pretend, but I couldn't fail. I refused to be that much of a slacker because in the back of my mind, when I logically thought ahead to what life could be like after I killed my father and escaped, I knew I would need a job. Obtaining a useful degree now could benefit me in the long run. Whenever I could have the freedom to work for a living and provide for Maxim, to make a life on my own terms, I would be able to use my college experience.

So pay attention and stop whining. I blinked and rubbed my eyes that were so irritated from the cold walk and lousy sleep. Buckling in to listen to Viktor's lecture, I forced myself to remain alert and do my work.

By the time he would speak to me this evening in his office about my makeup work, I would be prepared, confident, and put-together again.

13

VIKTOR

Irina was stubborn. I could count on her to have an attitude about having to report to my office, but I couldn't tell whether she would obey me. Yesterday, she'd seemed turned on about my claim that I'd punish her for wasting my time. The thought of her craving my dominance made her even more irresistible. But I couldn't guess if she'd show up this evening like I asked her to.

The internal debate of *will she, won't she?* plagued me all day. I couldn't stop thinking about her and wondering if she would show up. I anticipated it, getting ahead of myself in imagining how much more I could push her and how much further I could test her limits.

She came, though, a couple of minutes earlier than when my official office hours would start.

"I told you not to waste my time, Irina."

She paused mid-step in entering my office, eyeing me carefully. "I heard you."

I got up from my desk and approached her. Brushing against her side, I gave her a heated look as I reached out to close the door. She dipped her chin, watching my hand on the doorknob. When I moved my finger over to flick the lock, she drew in a deep breath. I refrained, though. Just teasing her about locking her in here with me was enough for now.

"Then why were you late this morning?" Still standing so close to her, I tortured myself with the scent of her sweet vanilla fragrance. It added to the forbidden nature of my attraction to her. She was so young, yet with an old soul. She was so pure and probably inexperienced, yet unafraid to show it. Tension ratcheted higher as we stayed within each other's space, not moving away from the closed door.

"I fail to see how the reason for my tardiness could be any of your business," she replied.

Aha. There she is. I wouldn't be seeing the glum and depressed version of this sexy woman. She was giving me the sass. The attitude. The defiance, and fuck if I wasn't all for it.

"It's always my business when my students decide to waste my time and treat my class as if it doesn't matter." Advancing toward her, I set her into a retreat. She backed up across the room as I walked toward her. Stalked her. She was my target. She would be my prey.

"To disrespect my class rules is to disrespect me."

She tipped her chin up, giving me a level glare. "That still doesn't mean you can demand to know why I was late."

"Why were you?" I asked again, glad when she backed up to my desk. Her legs bumped into the piece of furniture, and she glanced down at the impact. "Tell me what was more important than coming to my class."

She licked her lips, taunting me with a hungry need to taste her there. No answer came from her lips as she stared at me.

"Who were you seeing?" I asked as I took another step toward her.

Nothing.

"What were you doing?"

Silence. It felt so heavy, but not awkward, as though this simmering attraction and tension was something we'd already embraced as a consistent variable in our lives.

"Too busy partying late all night?" I taunted, relishing the pressure of her body nearly flush to mine. With my desk behind her, she had nowhere to go. Nowhere to turn or hide. Yet, with her sullen silence and refusal to answer me, she remained as elusive and closed-lipped as ever.

"You won't win at this game, Irina."

She raised her brows. "What game?"

"You won't beat me at this. I will have my answers."

Tilting her head to the side, she narrowed her eyes. "Why does it matter? Why do you need to know a single thing about what I do outside of the time I'm in your classes?"

"I don't need to know," I said, almost contradicting myself with my curiosity about what she had been up to. My mission here was to find out all I could from her. But it seemed that seducing her was the only way to really reach her. I had to get her back to that looser stance she'd had when I was flirting with her yesterday.

She opened her lips to speak again, but I set my hand on my desk, slanting over her as I cupped her face. My moves robbed her of speech. She sucked in a breath as I stared into her bright blue eyes. Stroking my thumb over the smooth satin of her cheek, I hesitated for just a moment to torment her.

"But I want to know," I growled.

Too weak to resist her, too impatient to taste her, I closed the distance between us. Pulling her chin up as I ducked my head toward her, I demanded she meet me in the middle for a kiss. The second my lips brushed over hers, I knew I was done for. Electric heat swamped me.

From the contact of her warm, wet lips beneath mine all the way down to my dick, I felt the potency of this kiss in every cell. With every fiber of my being, through every rapid beat of my heart, I felt this kiss in a way I never had before.

A slight muffled sound of surprise left her mouth, but she didn't back up. Freezing for a millisecond, she let me press my lips against her. Then she answered. Reaching up, thrusting forward, she kissed me back.

Unbelievable.

She had no experience. I felt the lack of it, and as I reeled from the shock that this was likely her first kiss, I struggled to believe it.

I'd counted on her being a virgin. But never kissed?

It was a stroke of fortune I almost felt blessed with.

I pulled back only to stare into her eyes. They were wide open, bright with interest as she stared back at me. And with a slight, soft exhale, I heard the desperation she tried not to show.

"I want to know you," I whispered softly, a breath away from her mouth before I kissed her again, harder, with my lips sealed over hers and my fingers cradling the back of her head. I held her in place to demand she learn how to mold to me. To show her how to kiss me back.

A louder noise of surprise left her this time. Again, I backed up to peer at her. "I want to know what makes you want to be so naughty, thinking you could show up late like that."

I kissed her again, thrilled when she took the initiative to kiss me back harder at once. Lowering my other hand to the desk, I forced my chest toward her until she reclined back over the desk. When I ended the kiss this time, I kept my head close to hers, placing small kisses along her jaw and nuzzling her.

"I want to know why the thought of my punishing you turns you on," I added.

"It doesn't—"

I cut off her lie, kissing her again. Demanding entrance to her mouth, I slid the tip of my tongue along hers, still too closed and naïve to open up to me. As I leaned over her, she caught herself from falling by reaching up to place her hands on my shoulders, then looping them around my neck. With her holding on like that, I could move my hands to her ass and hoist her up on my desk.

"I told you not to waste my time, sweetheart."

Desire darkened her eyes as she panted, looking up at me. That endearment seemed to really hit a spot with her, and I felt like a wicked god to have that trick in my arsenal. She hugged me as I smoothed my hands along her thighs, encouraging her to part them wider as I stood as close as I could to the edge of my desk. The pressure of leaning against the wood was a paltry relief of friction against my erection trapped in my pants.

"And I don't want you to waste my time with lies, either," I scolded. "Don't deny me the truth I ask of you. You can't hide your arousal."

She opened and closed her mouth, seeming to struggle for a reply.

"The thought of me punishing you, of me correcting your disobedience. It turns you on."

"I..." She settled on huffing in disagreement.

"Don't deny it." I kissed her, sliding my tongue past her lips to devour her and explore. To absorb the shocking perfection of tasting her and feeling the soft velvet heat of her mouth. "Don't deny that you want this."

"I—" She panted, shaking her head as I slid my hands to her ass, pushing her against the erection tucked under the layers of my pants.

"You are desperate for me, sweetheart. Don't deny it."

"I don't…" Her brow furrowed as she sought my mouth for a kiss, proving herself wrong.

"You are." I angled my head to get a deeper seal of a kiss, reveling in the liquid-hot desire that filled me with her eager response.

"But I don't—" She tried to catch her breath. "I shouldn't—"

"Oh," I growled, loving how forbidden this was. "We really shouldn't." I lifted my hand toward the front of her, tracing over her smooth skin between her ass, thigh, and panty-covered pussy. "I shouldn't want to rip these off you." I stroked my fingers over the damp fabric, already coated by her cream.

She gasped, staring at me with absolute lust until we kissed again.

"And you shouldn't be this soaked," I added, twisting my fingers until the thin lace snapped.

Again, I cut her off from speaking with another drugging kiss.

"We shouldn't even be thinking about this." I hinted at where I wanted this to go, rubbing my fingertips over her cream-slickened entrance, teasing that I wanted to penetrate her there.

She jerked at my touch. "Professor—"

"Viktor," I corrected as I pushed my fingertip into her tight, wet entrance. "You call me by my name when I have your cunt sucking me in like this."

She breathed faster, closing her eyes as I kissed along her neck. Aiming for the sensitive flesh under her ear, I added another finger, thrusting them into her virgin pussy.

"You shouldn't be letting me touch you like this, Irina," I reminded her.

"But I want..." She moaned as I moved my thumb over her clit. Her legs parted wider as her head dropped back.

"Oh, I know what you want. But I shouldn't give it to you, right?"

She pouted, furrowing her brow as I straightened, keeping my fingers inside her.

"You shouldn't..." she agreed weakly. "But..."

"But you want it." I urged her to lean back a little on the desk, showing her with my free hand how she should rest her hand on the surface. "You want me to touch you." I kissed her before lowering to sit in my chair. "You want me to kiss you." I scooted the chair closer until I could kiss her bare knee. Her tall stockings revealed that bit of skin, but when I flipped her skirt up, she was bare for me.

"Viktor," she said, startled.

"You want me to taste you, don't you?" I taunted as I dipped my head toward her. Placing a kiss above the spot where my fingers disappeared into her, I stared up at her.

Her mouth hung open as she watched me. Shock and elation warred in her blue gaze, but most of all, her desire shone clearly.

"You shouldn't want me to," I growled before dragging my tongue around my fingers speared inside her. "I shouldn't fantasize about doing this."

She licked her lips and whimpered in need. "We shouldn't," she agreed weakly.

I grinned, loving that she could be so naughty to admit this was wrong at the same time she would make no move to stop me.

"But we will." I licked and sucked at her, never looking away. "I'm going to eat this sweet pussy until you come."

She spread her legs wider, her gaze hazy with lust, her cheeks flush with arousal.

"And you're going to hold my head and fuck my mouth," I ordered. Licking at her slit as I rubbed her clit, I waited for her to do that. Her fingers threaded through my hair until she had a good grip. One hand remained behind her as she propped herself up. And with jerky movements at first, she pushed her pussy at my mouth. Between her hand on my head and her hips arching toward my face, she participated in this oral scene we really, *really* never should have started.

"Just like that, sweetheart," I praised before smashing my face to her cunt. Her scent. Her taste. The sounds of her whimpers and my juicy sucks. The feel of her fingers trembling over my head. I was overwhelmed by all my senses concentrated on her.

"Fuck my face, Irina. Show me what a bad girl you are, fucking your professor's face."

She gasped, humping me faster as I sucked and licked harder.

"Keep these legs spread wide." I reached up to grab her thighs, forcing them apart. The shift in my angle jolted her, but she didn't let go. She fell back on the desk, dropping her arm that she was leaning with.

The sight of her lying on my desk, her legs draped over the edge, was just too much for me to stand. She couldn't hump up at my face as well anymore, but I could pin her to the desk better this way. With her fingers locked in my hair, I stayed put and sucked on her hard clit until she cried out.

She squirted, coating my chin with more of her cream, but I was too greedy to wait. Before she could come down from her high, I stood and reached for my pants. There was no way in hell I could deny myself any longer. I set out to seduce her, but I'd tortured myself too hard.

"You shouldn't have," I told her, taking in the sight of her trembling from coming. "You shouldn't have let me do that." I unzipped then pulled her toward the edge of the desk. "I shouldn't have started that."

She shook her head weakly but said, "Uh-huh."

"Because now I want more."

Just before I could pull my dick out of my pants, the sound of metal clicking against metal reached me. The doorknob was spinning. Someone was entering my office.

She heard it too, jackknifing to sit upright. I shifted to the side, hiding her bare pussy still quivering from her orgasm. I blocked the sight of her skirt flipped up.

Wiping my chin and licking my lips, I tried to hide the evidence of what I was up to with my student in here.

Our trespasser likely knew what was going on anyway. Jessica stood in the open doorway, her hand still on the doorknob. She was the one who'd interrupted us. She was the one who just had to pop in and act like she had any welcome in this private space.

Irina held her breath, sitting there unmoving, while Jessica volleyed her gaze between me and her.

One thin red brow jumped up. "What's going on here?" she asked in a coy, teasing tone that proved she knew damn well what I was up to with Irina.

Fuck.

14

IRINA

The tall redhead narrowed her eyes at me, no doubt recognizing me from when I saw her here, in this same office, attempting to kiss Viktor.

My position on his desk and the way he stood between my legs was awfully damning evidence that she'd caught us doing a lot more than kissing. It wasn't proper. It shouldn't have happened. But weak and carried away by the foreign excitement of a man paying attention to me in such a way that felt so good, I caved.

"My bad." She smirked, parroting my words that I'd spoken when I caught her with Viktor. "I didn't realize this was a private moment."

"It doesn't matter what kind of a moment this is," he stated sternly, quickly twisting to face her fully at the same time he flipped my skirt all the way down over my thighs. I clamped them together, feeling so naughty when I missed the presence of my panties between them. He'd ripped them, yanked them right off me!

"You are trespassing, again, Ms. Nolan."

I frowned, piecing together who this woman might be. *Nolan?* I'd just learned of that name. My father mentioned it. Owen Nolan, the dean. Panic started to hit me that someone high up could've walked in on an inappropriate activity between a student and a professor.

"I like it when you call me Jessica," she complained.

"Ms. Nolan," he repeated, ignoring her wishes, "I don't care who your uncle is—"

"The dean," she reminded him curtly, crossing her arms. "He's the *dean.*"

"Dean or not," Viktor replied, "you have no right to try to insert yourself into my life."

"But one of your students can?" She lifted one arm from over the other to flick her finger at me in a scornful point.

"Get out," he ordered.

Even though he was facing her and clearly telling her to leave, I took his instruction to heart. Shame filled me. Humiliated and anxious to be caught in such a compromising situation, I damned this blush that heated my cheeks as I jumped off the desk. Feeling air between my legs in the absence of my panties, I was reminded with my every movement of how naughty I'd been with him. The slickness of my arousal and his saliva only drove that memory in deeper.

I was getting out of here before I'd erupt in a blush or stammer something I shouldn't say. I had no clue *what* to say or do. But running felt smart. It seemed like a natural instinct. In the name of fight or flight, I could either face off with the dean's niece or get the hell out of here.

I chose option two. Without looking at either of them, I grabbed my coat and bag from the chair and edged past Jessica. She didn't budge as I fled, looking down her nose at me as I scrambled. Only once I was out in the hallway then turning the corner to run down another did I let myself fully suck in a breath.

Shock chased me all the way back to my apartment. I couldn't believe that had happened. That we'd both been rebels and gone for something taboo and forbidden. Acknowledging how wrong it was to act on our mutual attraction for each other made it all the more wicked. He'd dismissed how bad it was to touch me, to kiss me, to nearly fuck me, and I had been right there alongside him, wanting it all.

But I refused to regret it. I couldn't. It was the first time a man kissed me. The first time I'd been touched. My first orgasm that I hadn't given myself. As I hurried home, my thighs rubbing against each other as a repeated reminder that he'd taken my panties off so roughly so he'd have access to me, I couldn't think it was bad.

If I had a chance to do it all over again, without a doubt, without hesitation, I would have.

Viktor had ruined me, making me want so much more with him. Surrendering to my desire for him meant I'd now feel this residual throb and ache between my legs. I'd relish the whisker burn of his stubble-covered jaw where he'd pushed his face at my pussy.

Because now that I felt how good it could be, how deliciously fulfilling it was to be wicked and sinful with him—my professor, a man so much older than me, and someone my father didn't know about—I wanted him again.

Even the shame of Jessica Nolan interrupting us and catching us nearly in the act couldn't make my desire for Viktor fade.

But the sight at the door to my apartment doused any trace of my arousal.

One guard stood there, as usual. His back to my closed door, he faced off with two men. I recognized them on sight. I knew Andre, but while I never learned the other Ilyin man's name, I knew what family he was affiliated with.

"What's going on?" I demanded as I strode forward.

I was sick of seeing these Ilyins. I was tired of my father's men in my presence too. All of them were examples of the life I wanted to escape.

"Just talking," my father's guard, Peter, said.

"Talking *here*?" I asked, making sure my tone was all business and demanding, not cutesy or inquisitive. I expected answers. I didn't need to look inviting or bubbly, forcing myself to be a popular extrovert to get them to warm up to me and gossip like I had to act around the students and staff on campus. These men knew damn well who I was. There was no point beating around the bush or keeping up pretenses.

Andre nodded, stroking his hand down his beard as he leered at me. His stare made me feel filthy, like I was a meal to engorge on then shove aside. When Viktor checked me out, he feasted his eyes on me like I was the answer to a famished man desperate for me and me alone. A prize. A reward. Something and someone to savor.

And he had. Just a half hour ago, on his desk, he had.

"Just talking. And checking in," Andre replied as he continued to stare at me.

Slightly nervous that he could smell a hint of sex on me or that he could somehow know that I'd done something sexy and naughty with another man, I kept my legs closer together and straightened. "Checking in with the guard of your rival?" I retorted.

"Rival?" Andre chuckled, still stroking his gangly beard. "I'm not sure that'll be true for long."

You wish. Igor Petrov would never form an alliance with the Ilyin Family. He could lie and cheat and con them into thinking they could be friends. It was why he'd helped the Ilyins capture Lev in some fake show of "the enemy of my enemy is my friend." My father was the one who'd set Yusef Ilyin's death into action, a kill Lev had completed. That hit was what made the Ilyins go after the Baranovs, and it was all in some part a duplicitous scheme orchestrated by my father.

"What the hell are you talking about?" I demanded. Glancing at Peter, I caught him smirking and rolling his eyes.

"I'm talking about how I figured I could stop by and check in on my future bride." Andre grinned, reaching out to caress my arm.

I swatted his hand away, stunned by his words but careful not to reveal how shocked I felt. "That's nonsense."

"No, it's not," Andre argued.

"Stop making up stupid shit like that," I warned with all the bravado I could manage. He tried again to feel my arm, and I shoved his hand away.

"I'm not." He smiled wider, as if my putting up a fight excited him. "According to what I heard, Igor Petrov promised that his one and only daughter would marry an Ilyin. May as well be *me*."

No. No fucking way. I refused to let those words sink into my conscious mind.

Absolutely fucking not.

My plan was to get the hell out of this life before I could be promised to someone. I had to kill my father then run with Maxim so we could finally have a life at all.

Andre didn't say anything else, chuckling at my shocked reaction of gaping at what he'd said. I couldn't help it. There was no way I could keep up a mask and hide my reactions to this news.

"See you soon, Wife," he said over his shoulder in farewell.

I stared after him, rooted in place with dread weighing down my stomach. The moment he was gone, I turned toward Peter. "What the fuck is that about? Promised to marry an Ilyin?"

He shrugged and shook his head, feigning ignorance. "First I heard about it."

"And you didn't think to tell him he had to be wrong?" They were our rivals! Or they were my father's rivals.

"I don't know if he is wrong," Peter argued. "No one can ever be one step ahead of the Boss or know what he's planning. Maybe this is how he'll get rid of you once and for all."

As a sacrifice to a rival? I shook my head, scared and angry at the possibility of it. *Over my dead body.* "Then let's go. Right now."

He scowled at me, not moving.

"Let's go to my father and ask him what the hell this is about."

"No. Not now." He checked his phone. "George told me that you need to go to a party off campus. Marcus Jameson might be there, and the Boss expects you to get some intel about him."

"Fuck this party." I pushed to get past him and enter my apartment.

"No, Irina," Peter ordered as he followed me inside. "You are to follow orders. The Boss told me to make sure you get to this party and find out what you can."

I growled, so frustrated and fed up with this that I flung my coat to the nearest chair, not caring whether it landed or fell to the floor.

"Then we can go talk to the Boss and you can ask him about any engagement he might've planned for you. You can tell him what you learn about at this party, too."

Lifting my head to stare at the ceiling, I fumed and counted to ten. That little trick hardly ever worked, but I tried my best to cram all my anxiety and disappointments back into a tidy little compartment and do as I was told.

Again.

15

VIKTOR

Jessica stared down Irina as she scrammed. I hated that Irina felt like she had to run. In the back of my mind and in the bottom of my heart, I entertained a fanciful thought that she'd stay. That she'd stick around and face off with Jessica. It would've been a sight to behold, Irina standing up to Jessica and staking her claim on me.

But it wasn't happening. Irina took off, her face so pink with an uncharacteristic blush at being caught with me. I couldn't blame her for reacting like that in this context. She was a virgin, and clearly, so unused to doing anything with a man that she lacked the experience of how to handle this kind of situation. I could hardly expect her to own up to her sexuality when she hadn't ever really embraced it before.

This too-bold and pain-in-the-ass redhead, though, she knew damn well what she was doing by interfering like this.

"This is the last time that I will tell you to leave me alone."

She sighed as though I were asking her to do something impossible.

"Do you understand me?"

"I suppose..." She smiled, coyly and too smugly for me to believe that she meant it. Turning slowly, she gave me a mischievous smirk as she left.

After she went away, I shut my office door and growled. This time, I locked the damn thing for real. The moment I spun and faced my desk, I groaned with need.

"Dammit."

I'd been so close to sinking into Irina's sweet little pussy. From sampling the pleasure I could get from being her first. The pride I would have in taking her V card.

But I hadn't. Jessica just had to show up and ruin it all.

I dragged my hand over my face, hating how this evening was turning out. I wouldn't admit that I'd failed. I had gotten her to relax around me. I did get her open up... or at least she'd opened her legs to me. What I hadn't gotten were any answers. She didn't tell me where she was last night or why she was late to class. Really, those answers couldn't matter in the big picture of what I needed to find out for Oleg. They did matter in the vein of getting her vulnerable enough to speak up and not be so secretive around me, though. If she couldn't tell me why she was late to class, what hope did I have to expect her to share any details about what Igor Petrov was planning?

I had one of two options now. I could chase her down, stop at her apartment, and pick up where we'd left off—if she'd let me. Or I could lurk and let her suffer under the pressure of this unfinished attraction that burned between us.

Either way might work. My seduction wasn't complete. It boiled down to the matter of whether I could wait and be patient.

With the way I still burned for her touch and sweet kisses, I wasn't sure I had it in me to wait for another chance to be alone with her.

My phone pinged with a text notification. The sound jarred me from my thoughts of what to do about Irina. Sighing, so frustrated that I didn't know what to do with myself, I picked it up and checked the screen.

Lev: *One of the men patrolling near one of the warehouses mentioned a party happening.*

"What the fuck is with all these goddamn parties?" I grumbled. I wasn't a fan of going out, most likely because for the last twenty years, I'd been working in one big orgy or party to the next. The whorehouses were like party central, and I'd tired of them.

Lev: *It sounds like the Ilyins and Petrovs are angling to have a meeting there.*

"Huh." I rubbed the back of my head, missing the tight grip of Irina's fingers in my hair.

Lev: *I doubt that's true, but since Rurik is tied up with something else, it might make sense for you to check it out.*

It wasn't an order. And Lev wasn't exactly my superior just yet. Still, I would do my job. The whole reason for me to be on campus and near Irina was to get intel about Igor Petrov's plans, not to mope and whine about my missed opportunity to sink my cock into her tight pussy.

"Yeah, yeah," I complained aloud as I stood. I texted him back that I'd check it out, and he texted me the address a moment later.

I headed to my apartment to clean up. Wearing the residue of Irina's cream on my face wasn't an issue, but I did want to change out of this proper and professional suit. I couldn't wear a damn tie to a party that dealers were setting up.

After a quick shower, where I jerked off to the memory of Irina on my desk just to calm myself from wanting her, I left for this party.

When I arrived, it was clear that I was getting there too late to really be able to notice who had been there. People were leaving, laughing and talking about bar hopping. It was either a lame party or just one of those things where people came and went. As I walked up to the place, more guests left and others came alongside me.

Deep bass of the music thumped and vibrated before I actually set foot in the apartment. Overhead, a disco ball spun in the entryway, its glittering lights competing with the snowflakes falling from the moonlit sky.

It was packed in here, and I tried to orient what was where. I had only come to scope the scene and report back to Lev, but I stopped short at the sight of something else.

Or rather, someone else.

Lev implied that I had to get myself into the position to listen in on or spy on a meeting between members of the Petrov and Ilyin Families, but I only saw one side.

Two Ilyin soldiers were in the corner of the large room. And both of them were in the middle of trying to drag a woman away with them. Fresh rumors about the Ilyins dispersing drugs and raping women would've made me suspicious of them, anyway. The fact that they were trying to force Irina to leave with them arrested me mid-step.

What the fuck?

I didn't think. No plans flew through my mind. Reacting on autopilot and driven on the instinct to reach her, I pushed and wove my way through the crowd to get to them.

I shoved people aside, making them freak out at spilling their drinks. I plowed past couples dancing, earning their shouts about watching where I was going.

I tuned it all out. The noise and chaos of the party faded in my mind's eye. My heart raced as I chased down the two men.

They'd gotten her outside before I could approach. Both men had their hands on her, grabbing her upper arms to force her out with them. She didn't go easily. Kicking and yelling, flailing to get free, she resisted them.

And that made no sense at all.

Where are her fucking guards?

Why is anyone even letting this happen?

I didn't ask any questions. I didn't announce a single thing. Coming up behind them, I acted swiftly and lethally. First, I pulled back the arm of the man at her right. He fought back, surprised that someone was getting to him, but I was faster.

"Let her go."

I swung first, getting him in the face and being rewarded with a satisfying grunt of pain. As soon as he flung back from my hit, the other man attacked. Neither of them released Irina until I beat on them some more. Two against one wasn't terrible odds, and within several minutes and a few lucky hits they snuck in on me, I had them down on the ground, moaning in pain and grimacing. One was only just coming to after I'd knocked him out with a brutal punch to the side of his head.

"Are you insane?" Irina asked, watching me closely as I straightened from the last hit I'd delivered.

The whole fight couldn't have lasted more than three minutes. It had started and finished with such a blur, but she was still there.

She hadn't run off scared. She didn't alert anyone to come to help, not even a Petrov who should've been watching her. She was a Boss's daughter. No matter the details of their family or organization, she was a Mafia princess who should've been protected at all costs.

"No." I winced, shaking out my hand as I staggered toward her. A few more seconds, and I'd be right again. The adrenaline rush of the fight waned, and the pain from the hits I'd received rushed in all at once.

"Those men…" She shook her head. "You can't just—"

"They were trying to take you away."

She narrowed her eyes at me. Even though she'd questioned my sanity, she hadn't asked it as a shriek or an alarmed shout. She was still cool and collected, almost as though she were numb to this kind of violence. She should be, as a Mafia princess. She wouldn't have grown up in a sheltered home where she could've been spared all this drama.

And I hated that.

She deserved better. Deep down, I knew that without being able to explain it.

"Those aren't just some college boys, Viktor." She walked toward me, watching me with a guarded but non-hysterical expression as I shook my hand then rubbed my side where I'd been hit. "They're dangerous men."

I played stupid, letting her think I was just an ordinary man, a college professor. Of course, I knew who those guys were. I identified them as Ilyin men right away, but I couldn't reveal that I was an insider to this Mafia world.

"And more of them are coming now," I warned, noticing more men filing out of the party.

I reached out for her hand, hurrying to run with her. Tugging her along, I half-expected her to protest. She didn't. Not once did she open her mouth to speak. No questions, no demands for me to stop.

As I got her to safety, returning to my car to get her in the passenger seat, she didn't question me at all.

I had so many questions for her that I didn't know where to start.

Why was she there unprotected?

What were those Ilyin men trying to steal her away for?

Weren't the Petrovs and Ilyins enemies after the business with Lev killing Yusef Ilyin?

"Viktor," she said once I drove off.

I glanced at her, scowling, but not *at* her. I didn't like the thought of her being manhandled or forced somewhere against her will. While I lacked the clues and details about what was going on there, I didn't like what I saw.

"Are you all right?" I reached over to check her arm, looking at her wrist where one of them had held on to her.

"Yes." She pulled her arm back. "I'm fine."

"Those men were trying to kidnap you."

She exhaled a long breath and looked out the passenger window. When she should've seemed scared or even mad, she appeared resigned instead. Like this was just fate and she didn't have the power to fight it.

And I hated it.

Irina was an enemy. She had to be an enemy of mine. The Petrovs and Baranov families were not friends, so therefore, as members of opposing sides, we had to be adversaries to an extent. Yet, the more I planned to seduce her and get close enough for her to talk to me, I was surprised with how much I wished things could be different.

That she could just be a woman I'd met and wanted so badly I ached to close my lips over hers again. That I could just be a man who'd noticed her and whom she wanted to welcome into her arms.

Because she had been born the daughter of Igor Petrov, though, she was my enemy.

Too many lines were getting blurred here. I wasn't supposed to want her. She wasn't supposed to get under my skin like this.

"I'm fine," she repeated, monotone and matter-of-fact about it, which didn't do a damn thing to convince me that she was anywhere close to fine after that incident. "It's complicated, but I'm fine."

"So I shouldn't have fought them off for trying to force you away with them?" I asked, trying and failing to not sound testy.

"No. I appreciate that," she replied, sincere but still resigned.

I frowned as I drove, nodding when she asked if I could just take her home. Listening to her give me the address, I pretended that I didn't already know that detail about her.

Silence filled the car, but I didn't mind it. I needed the quiet. With her company, I could attest to her being safe. During the silence, I mulled over the realization that I wanted to comfort her and see to her safety —not target her as someone who possessed secrets the Boss wanted me to pry out of her. I wrestled with the urge to pull over and just hold her. I ignored the reminder that I should be doing my duty to interrogate her and intimidate her into telling me family secrets.

Every time I glanced at her, I saw how scared she was. She wasn't fine. Despite her cool mask, I picked up on enough clues that told me she was frightened and bothered by those two Ilyin men trying to get her away.

I hated that she'd feel like this. But like she'd pointed out, this was complicated, getting messier by the minute as I considered the very real possibility that I had already started to care too much for her than what was wise.

16

IRINA

Viktor dropped me off and waited until I got into my building before driving off. I couldn't be sure what his game was with me. I also couldn't begin to guess why he'd been at that party. It was in an even seedier part of town than the other one where I saw him.

A professor going down on his student in his office was scandalous enough. But his happening to show up at a party I was supposed to spy at, then rescuing me from men who thought they could do as they wanted with me?

Weird.

I called everyone I could in my father's employ to reach him. He wasn't answering his phone, but that didn't stop me from calling nonstop.

Leave it to him to be unreachable when I would be demanding an explanation for why Andre Ilyin or anyone else in that family would think that I'd be arranged in a marriage with them.

Finally, after hours of pacing in my apartment, Peter knocked on my door. I opened it to glare at him. "The Boss is not available to take a call tonight."

I glowered at him even more. "Tell me something I don't know." I already knew he wasn't answering.

"But I asked around and it sounds like this is just a rumor." He shrugged and rubbed his chin. "Maybe it's all bullshit." He hadn't confirmed nor denied what Andre said when he'd stopped by my place.

"A rumor?" I huffed, not buying that. Rumors could be spread and machinated for any number of reasons. Lies were a common currency many in the Mafia used. But that explanation didn't add up after what happened at that party. Those two Ilyin men hadn't been joking around when they came up and told me I was going home with them. That was no rumor or prank. They'd meant it.

But my father wasn't available to explain why a rival family would be following a rumor about an arranged marriage with me. He wasn't available that night, nor at any time the next day and night. I had to struggle with the unknown for two whole days. It set me in a constant state of anxiety to the point that I stayed in my apartment and didn't dare to leave.

Rumor or not, if an Ilyin spotted me and tried to whisk me away, I couldn't count on my father's men to care. They wouldn't know whether it was a legitimate deal or not. They didn't give a damn about me to begin with, seeing me as a problem, not a relative. No one had come to that party—my driver had just dropped me off and left me on my own.

The idea of marrying an Ilyin, Andre or not, felt like a death sentence. I didn't want to marry a rival. Doing so would ensure my life would always be a business transaction. There would be no end to the drama and politics. I didn't want to marry a Mafia man at all.

Marriage was the last thing on my mind now, especially after meeting Viktor. He'd made me come. He'd saved me. He seemed to care. Even though I couldn't discern why he cared, he did, and that meant a lot to me after a lifetime of being used or neglected, stuck between those wild extremes.

If I was expected to get married, I couldn't begin to guess what that would mean for Maxim. I was the only one looking out for him. If I belonged to a husband, Igor wouldn't have power over me anymore. What would that result in for my brother? Would Igor just kill him? He would have no incentive to toe the line and provide for him if I could no longer be his spy.

Wait a second.

Another dreadful idea hit me when finally, two nights after I heard about my supposed engagement, I was on the ride to his house.

What if he's making me marry an Ilyin so I can spy further in depth, in their house and in their family?

The prospect of being a pawn and a spy forever would be enough to drive me to suicide.

I didn't wait for the driver to open my door after we arrived. I strode inside, seeking out my father who couldn't be bothered to answer his phone for two fucking days when his daughter called. He had probably been shacked up with one of his mistresses, acting like a lord and getting pampered.

"Why would anyone in the Ilyin family act as though I am to be married to one of their men?"

That was my greeting. I crossed my arms, cutting straight to the matter at hand.

He grunted, pausing while eating his dinner. Enough food was splayed out on the table for six people, but he was a gluttonous asshole to waste it all on himself. "How polite you are these days. No hello."

"Fuck manners, Igor." I didn't care if he disliked my tone. "Answer me."

He grunted, rolling his eyes. I expected him to bristle at my attitude, to tell me to watch it. He must have been amused by my question, though, because he cleared his throat and wiped his mouth with a napkin in preparation to speak. "I didn't directly say anything on that matter."

Bullshit. This rumor had to have started somewhere. My level glare told him what I thought of his comment.

"I may or may not have let some rumors get carried away, though."

Ah-ha.

"But it doesn't matter for you, anyway. Whether you're arranged to marry or not, you will not act any differently." He lifted his head, tipping his chin up as he narrowed his eyes. "I expect you to remain a virgin for your husband. Whenever I do choose one, whoever I decide upon, you *will* be untouched. Because that fact should not change, so what does it matter if the Ilyins want to amuse themselves and run with this idea?"

Just when I thought I couldn't have hated him more.

"Let them think what they want," he said, lowering his gaze and shrugging. "One day, I will be the one and only main boss in this area. I will then call all the shots and have every say over any rumors that originate."

He's just playing games. That's all this is to him. This diabolical asshole was playing a game with my life, with my future. "Tell me the truth. Am I or am I not promised to anyone?"

He looked at me like I was being silly to want to know. Resuming his dinner, he barely paid me any attention.

"The Ilyin men are trying to capture me. They attempted to at that party you wanted me to go to."

He shrugged. "If they attempt it, then you will be retrieved as I see fit."

I narrowed my eyes, lost in how he could order me to remain a virgin but also turn the other way and ignore what could happen to me if I were captured by a rival.

"Am I promised to anyone!" It was a question, but I couldn't frame it as one, too angry to stand still. Fisting my hands at my sides, I fought the urge to leap over the table and throttle him. Let him choke on his dinner. "Am I promised to an Ilyin?"

He scoffed, relenting at last to answer me. "Of course not." He let out an exasperated sigh. "Of course, I don't want you married to one of those idiots."

You fucking asshole! He could've just told me that first. He could've answered directly, but no. He had to fuck with me and play mind games just for his enjoyment, just to peeve me.

"Why would I want you married to the losers I want to push out of power?"

I didn't reply, seething and too furious to speak.

"Just play along with it. In fact, ignore it. Don't even speak about this. Do as I ask, and that's it." His expression hardened once more. "Do as I tell you and spy on that campus. That's all you need to worry about. And if you give a shit about that worthless brother of yours, I can count on you to do your duty."

I stared him down, damning him for ever taking advantage of my love for Maxim.

"Are more drugs being circulated?" he asked. "Are there new dealers after the Ilyins' last shipment to the area?"

I didn't reply.

He pounded his fist on the table, but I didn't jump, used to his dramatics. "Answer me!"

"No."

He stood. "No, you're not going to answer me?"

"No, to the best of my knowledge, there are not any new drugs being traded or sold."

"What about Marcus James and Eric Benson? Is anyone trying to get any favors with the dean's office?"

I hadn't even tried to snoop there. And I didn't want to. With him pressing me for answers, all I wanted to do was run. Run far and fast and never stop. This wasn't the life I wanted.

Without another word, I turned and stormed off. Enveloped in fury, I walked right back out front where the driver was still standing outside the car, smoking a cigarette.

"Already?" he asked.

As if I'd ever want a visit here to be long. "Yes. Can we leave?"

He shrugged, tossing his cigarette then smashing it with his shoe on the icy pavement.

I got in the backseat and asked, "Can I go visit Maxim?"

"He said no. Until further notice."

I fisted my hands again, uncaring how my arms vibrated and tremored with the force of my muscles being used. I was so desperate to feel some hope. Some love or minor concern. More than anything, I craved the security and consideration I felt when Viktor helped me at the party. The deep pleasure and shocking relief when he'd made me come in his office.

I wasn't on the hunt for naughtiness with him. I was just so sick of feeling this loathing, this hatred and rage. It was consuming me, from the inside out.

I'd never been so mad at Igor, stunned that he would play a game like this to lead the Ilyins on. He'd let them think I'd marry into their family when he had zero intention of ever letting it happen.

I stared out the window, fuming, but I couldn't be too upset about not seeing Maxim at this hour. It was late for him. But I couldn't just simmer and sulk at my apartment, left to nothing but an idle mind and too much anger.

After I was dropped off, I grabbed my tote bag and walked to the library. Reading and studying probably wouldn't solve anything, but I was that eager to get out and do something before I drove myself insane.

17

VIKTOR

I didn't see Irina for two days. She didn't show up to her poetry class. There were no signs of her at her usual haunts, the café, the cafeteria, the coffee shops, the library, and the gym. I didn't spot her once.

Aggravated that I was so hung up on her, I tried to talk myself down from missing her. She couldn't matter like that. Sure, she had the sweetest pussy I'd ever tasted, but she was still a target to spy on. A source to get intel from. A Mafia princess from a rival family.

I also did my best not to worry. I delivered her back to her apartment in one piece, and I knew she had to have guards there. Going back to her place and checking on her was next on my list, but I wanted to be patient. She had to be suspicious of my interest as it was, and I didn't want to risk her getting more suspicious or curious.

By the end of the second day, I felt like I'd go crazy if I bottled in all this worry and confusion. So, I headed back to the Baranov mansion, accepting an invitation to dinner with the Boss, Lev, and Eva. Boris was there too, but like always, Oleg's younger brother didn't speak much, just drinking into oblivion.

LEONA WHITE

I stopped at the main whorehouse on my way there, checking in on how things were going with the man I'd had working in my stead. I was sure I'd be stuck going back there eventually, so it would probably pay off to keep in touch with how things were going.

After dinner, Eva commiserated with my report. "I'm not surprised you're struggling to get close to her."

"I didn't say I was struggling, per se…"

She smiled as she rolled her eyes. "However you want to say it. Irina never seemed to have many friends. Not real ones. She's always seemed like someone who refrained from letting anyone in."

But why? Eva was sort of the same, held to a higher standard in the society of the Mafia organizations because she was a Mafia princess. She proved that she could make friends, though, like she had with that Kelly woman for a while.

"It's curious that the Ilyins were trying to capture her," Oleg said, puffing on his after-dinner cigar.

Lev nodded. "I can't see Igor being too pleased with the Ilyins if they'd succeeded."

Neither could I, but I witnessed them trying to capture her. It had happened, for whatever reason.

I enjoyed my time with them, but all too soon, it was time for me to go. If I didn't see Irina tomorrow, I'd seek her out at her place.

On the drive back to my apartment, still in my suit and tie since I hadn't changed after working on papers and crap for the next lecture, plus spying on some Petrov soldiers who were loitering near the gym, my phone buzzed with a text from Rurik. I checked the screen at a light.

Rurik: *I heard you were trying to find your girl.*

I huffed. "My girl?" I could hardly claim Irina was mine. I did miss the pleasure on her face when I called her *sweetheart*, though.

Rurik: *I just spotted her heading to the library. I was there watching Kelly for a while.*

"Huh." I found it curious that Oleg and Lev still had Rurik doing checks on the blonde friend Eva had made. Kelly hadn't reached out to Eva at all, but Oleg and Lev seemed to want to offer slight protection and courtesy checks on the woman, hence why Rurik was on campus when he was.

Viktor: *Thanks.*

I was slightly surprised that she'd go to the library this late, but as I'd learned on my previous stops there, the old building of books seemed busier after the sun went down.

I parked and headed there, shoving my hands as deep as they could go in my pockets. I was sick of this weather. Spring could come and thaw us any time now.

After I entered the four-story library, I set out to hunt her down. She wasn't in any of the study areas where I sometimes spotted her, but I hit the jackpot on the top floor. Large windows showed the snow drifting down outside on the square. While the vista could've been picturesque, Irina was seated further from the windows.

As I strolled toward her, she sighed and shook her head. Then she stood, stretching a little before carrying a book back to a shelf.

Following behind her, I paused at her table and draped my coat over hers. It'd be fine there as I stalked her down the long aisles of books. While the lower levels had more students—some studying and some seeming to jam to music and just talk—she must have chosen this top floor for the quiet. Hardly anyone was up here, and I relished the illusion of privacy I could have with her.

LEONA WHITE

She didn't turn or acknowledge me as I followed her, and I wondered what could be weighing down her mind so much that she wasn't paying attention to her surroundings. Growing up in a Mafia family, she'd have better street smarts than most women.

Flinching a little at seeing me closing in on her down a long aisle between tall cases laden with books, she raised her brows in surprise. "Viktor," she greeted.

God, I missed her voice. I slowed, walking up to her and taking the book out of her hand. It was a text for rock formations. "Are you burning the midnight oil cramming for a geology exam?" I guessed.

She shrugged, lowering her gaze as she looked at the book in my hand.

"Is that why I haven't seen you anywhere on campus these last couple of days? You've been too busy studying?"

Lifting her face to me, she slyly smiled, as though the idea of my looking for her pleased her. Excited her. "You've noticed my absence?"

How could I not?

"Oh, let me guess. You're just pissed that I missed the poetry class today."

"I'm not mad..."

"You did tell me not to waste your time and disrespect the class rules and expectations," she teased mildly.

"I did. But every student is allotted two missed days before their grade is affected." *But you don't care about your grade, do you?*

"What are you doing here, then?" I asked.

"I just wanted to come somewhere... safe."

Alarms sounded in my mind. I was instantly on edge with her

comment. I hated that she would ever feel in danger, and as soon as I acknowledged that, I wanted to groan.

She's supposed to be a target. The enemy.

"And being around all these old books makes me feel safe." She wrapped her arms around herself in a hug as she looked around at the rows and stacks of books surrounding us. Before she could elaborate, she continued walking further down the aisle, and beholden to needing and wanting her company, I followed behind.

"Thank you, by the way, for helping me out with those guys at that party."

I hadn't been counting on a heartfelt thanks, days later.

"They were just joking around."

I frowned at her. "Don't lie," I warned. "They were trying to kidnap you. Capture you."

She looked to the side, not commenting.

"Did you *want* them to capture you?" *Was it supposed to be some kind of ploy that I'd interrupted?* I felt like I was in the dark with what Igor had planned.

"No," she mumbled, furrowing her brow at me, as if I were an idiot to guess that. "Besides, what would it matter what *I* want?"

I smirked. She was a Mafia princess. She had to want for nothing.

"Tell me."

She stopped, facing me fully. "What?"

"Tell me what you want." I waited, calm and patient even though my blood boiled at hearing her fantasies or wishes.

Trapped under her stare, I felt like I was the luckiest man alive. To be the object of her attention. To see her blue eyes glittering with mischief.

Without losing eye contact with me, she smiled slightly, backing up a step. Then two. I advanced after her, curious whether she was literally trying to play a game of catch. The thought of her enjoying the thrill of a chase made me start to get hard.

"I want..." She swept the tip of her tongue along her lower lip. I couldn't get enough of this daring side of her.

I uncuffed my sleeves and rolled them up slowly, forcing myself to be patient before she'd tell me.

"I wish you'd kiss me again."

Fuck yes. I nodded, letting her see how much I desired her as I kept walking after her. She led us further into the maze of bookcases, securing our privacy from the center part of the library space.

"That you'd pick up right where you left off in your office," she added, her voice soft and quiet, as though she couldn't believe she was speaking her mind.

"That's what I want."

I tilted my head, prolonging this wait and letting the tension and suspense build between us. Because the moment I had her in my arms, I would be doing my best not to rush.

"I should punish you for such naughty thoughts about me, sweetheart. Lusting after your professor?" I shook my head slowly, taunting her.

She drew in a quick breath as her eyes darkened. Under the shadows this far into the library, she looked more exotic, more like an untouchable dream.

"Do it," she taunted. "Punish me. Make me *feel* something other than..." She frowned, focusing on me again. Reaching forward to grip my red tie, she stared at me with such a begging, pleading expression that I'd never be able to tell her no. I didn't intend to.

"I want you, Viktor," she whispered as she tugged on my tie, pulling me closer.

18

IRINA

Something had taken over me, making me act this bold and wanton. No one ever asked me what I wanted, so that alone was the ultimate turn-on. Seeing Viktor's face change from the bad-boy smirk and smile to the wicked lover's grin was more than enough to drive up my arousal.

"I want… you," I repeated, feeling stronger with each time I let that taboo statement leave my mouth.

"You want me to punish you for having such filthy thoughts about me?" he asked, lowering his hands to set them on my waist. The heaviness of his warm touch grounded me. It lured me in.

I nodded, unable to speak with my heart racing and my lungs not filling fast enough. His smoldering stare teased me. His low, gruff voice was like another caress on my skin. And his fingers flexed at my waist, testing out his grip to the point that I wanted him to clutch me and never let go. "Yeah, that's what I want."

He shook his head. "No." Stepping forward once more, he trapped me against the wall of bookcases behind me. "I'm not going to punish you. Not tonight." One more step pinned me in place. Thick and hard, his thigh wedged between mine, rubbing where I ached for him. "But I could fuck you."

I gasped as he kissed me, hard, fast, and brutal. There was no forgiveness in this rough press of his lips against mine. This wasn't a delicate moment of him pursuing me. He was taking. Demanding. Requesting without mercy.

Parting my lips, I let him in and tried to keep up with his lips and tongue. He dominated me, ordering me to open up and match this feral urgency he showed me.

His words were a live brand of desire on my soul, and I clutched him before I could rise up in flames. Holding on to his tie, I clung to him. He lowered his big hand until he cupped my ass, and with a quick, tight squeeze, he prompted me to raise my leg and wrap it around him so he could grind against me more effectively.

"I could fuck you, sweetheart. Right here. Right now."

Yes. Please, yes. I moaned, needy and greedy, hanging on to him and kissing him back for all I was worth.

I could trust that my father didn't want me married off to anyone in the Ilyin family, but this recent talk about my virginity had me wishing I could take charge of that one thing. That *I* could decide whom I gave it to.

And I wanted it to be Viktor.

Even if that meant we'd have sex right here, right now, in the library.

"Can you be quiet?" he taunted, laying a line of wet, sucking kisses down along my neck.

I let my head fall back, giving him access as I uttered a breathy *yes*. But then he tugged my blouse and bra cups down, popping the buttons off the thin shirt. He closed his mouth over my breast and sucked hard, making me cry out in dual parts shock and pleasure. "Oh, my God!" I put my hand on the back of his head to keep him there, but he moved back.

"No," he observed. "No, you can't be quiet." Kissing me again, he lowered his hand to my skirt, shoving it up until he could twist his fingers on my wet panties so slick with my juices. Just like before, he removed my lingerie with a quick rip. And without delay, he rubbed over my entrance before shoving his finger inside me.

With his mouth over mine, my moans of pleasure were muffled. All too soon, he pulled back, breathing hard. "Take my tie off," he ordered, kissing me again and trusting me to do as he said. I did, fumbling more than I wanted to. I was anxious and excited. I was nervous yet confident. I wanted him. I wanted to give him my virginity, no one else. But this was my first time, and my clumsiness and lack of experience showed.

As soon as I had his deep-red tie off, he broke the kiss. He lifted his hands to wrap the tie around my head. Gagging me. Silencing me. It felt risky to trust him like this, but I was so turned on and eager to give him my virginity that I couldn't think of protesting. I stared at him, mesmerized by the lust shining in his eyes, until he turned me.

"I can fuck this tight little pussy, sweetheart," he whispered into my ear. Shoving me up against the bookcase, he forced me forward. My breasts rubbed against the spines of the books, and the leather chafed my nipples, bared from his tugging my shirt and bra so low. He pulled my hips back, though, making sure I felt the hard ridge of his erection he had yet to get out. The slight touch of him near my pussy had me moaning, but with his tie stuck around my mouth, the noise was minimal.

I couldn't be loud. Anyone could hear if they were on this floor. And if someone were to come by, they'd see me, so much of me.

"You want me to stuff my cock in here?" He pumped his fingers into my body, smearing the cream that gushed out.

I nodded, hanging my head low as I held on to the edge of a shelf. Thrusting back to him helped ease the need. I rode his hand as he shifted to unzip his pants. The swish of his zipper sounded overly loud in this quiet building, but he didn't seem worried. Before I could get too close to coming, he withdrew his fingers and lined his dick up to me.

The bulbous cockhead stretched me at the entrance, but he waited for me to suck it in. Holding me still, he cupped my tits and kissed my neck.

When I couldn't handle the wait, I arched my back and willed him to drive into me. To fuck me, like he'd teased me that he would. To fill me so I wouldn't be so empty and spiraling with hopelessness and hatred for Igor Petrov, my father whom I would kill.

"So naughty," he growled between kisses. His fingers never stopped, tweaking my nipples and playing with my breasts. But down there, he slammed his big, long dick into me, making me flinch at the shock of the stretch.

He was all the way in, to the hilt. In one swift push, he had filled me, cramming that cock into me. No other man had ever touched me there. No other guy would ever have the privilege of being my first.

Viktor was. And as he slowly pulled out to slide back in, he proved that he'd fuck me so well that I couldn't bear to think about having another man in me like this.

Over and over, he pounded into me. Holding my waist but alternating by moving his hands back up to play with my breasts that felt so heavy and sensitive as they bounced and swayed from his thrusts, he controlled all the points of pleasure that I could rely on to feel so good.

Between his kisses on my neck and the eventual slide of his finger toward my clit, which he thrummed and rubbed in time with his deep thrusts, I was a goner.

I held on to the shelf's edge, not bothering to concern myself with how the metal structure squeaked and whined under the motion of Viktor fucking me so hard and fast.

That slight pinch of pain that came when he first slammed into me was long gone. Now, in its place, mounting pleasure electrified me.

Until I came, until I felt like I was exploding and shattering, letting bliss and utter relief claim me. He'd already given me one intense orgasm in his office, with his hands and mouth, but that was nothing like this. I felt fried and burned alive, so overcome with pleasure that I couldn't stand it.

Behind the tie gagging my mouth, I cried out and sobbed at the powerful release. Tears streaked down my face, wetting the fabric of the smooth tie. They were evidence of how strongly I felt this once-in-a-lifetime occasion, losing my virginity to the professor I wasn't supposed to want.

Before I could fully start to come down from the first waves of my climax, he drilled into me deeper yet. Far into me, he jerked and twitched. His dick pulsed, and I moaned again at the thought of his hot cum flooding my womb.

He shouldn't have come in me. I shouldn't have asked him to fuck me.

We shouldn't have caved.

But now that we had, I hung loose in his hug, catching my breath through my nose the best I could. Trembles raced through me, my body so sensitive to having sex for the first time. He noticed, always so quick to watch me and wait for my cues. Placing tender kisses along my neck, he sighed and accepted this crash from the rush of sex.

If he let me go now, I'd drop to the floor.

He didn't. Embracing me, keeping his long shaft inside me, he waited until we could both stand steadily.

I wasn't sure *when* reality would feel steady or consistent after he'd fucked me so thoroughly, but I would forever keep this night precious in my memories. There would be Before Viktor and After Viktor, and those generalizations of time would not be the same.

I would never be the same.

Tonight, I'd acted on what I wanted.

The night that I decided who I wanted to give my V card to.

Viktor, the professor I shouldn't have fallen for at all.

19

VIKTOR

I held Irina close to me, wishing I could feel all of her luscious, soft skin. Until she could stand steadier, I would keep her upright. Nuzzling her neck as I caught my breath, I tugged the cups of her bra back up to contain her huge tits. She shivered under my touch, still so hazy from coming hard with me. It felt like a crime to cover her up at all, but if someone came by and saw her, gagged and her shirt wide open, I'd want to murder them.

Irina was mine.

She had wanted to give her virginity to me, no one else. I felt like a fucking caveman, a god, a rabid lover who could rut her all over again. She chose me, not anyone else. Me.

My dick was still in her where we were glued together by our combined cum. And I made no move to pull out of her as I forced her shirt back together, fastening whatever buttons were left. She was hardly decent, but nothing was revealed.

Slowly, hating that I had to end this, I slid out of her and tucked my wet dick back into my pants. Then as I turned her around, I made sure her skirt flapped down and stayed in place.

I watched her as I loosened the knot in the tie that I'd used as a gag for her. Wearing suits and ties wasn't something I did often. After this gig was up, when I wouldn't need my cover anymore, I wouldn't think about ties again.

This tie, though, was now my favorite. I removed it fully from her face and tucked it into my pocket to savor later. The scorching hot memory of what we did would take a long time to fade. And this tie was my trophy, my collectible to commemorate it.

She heaved out a deep sigh, staring at me. Before she could speak, I heard the sounds of people walking nearby.

Fuck.

I kissed her, to keep her quiet. But no one passed us by. No one entered this aisle.

"Let's get out of here before we're interrupted again," I said, not really joking about how Jessica had just popped in that one day.

I spoke too soon, though, because the sounds of people walking in a closer aisle came next.

Irina opened her eyes wide with panic, then stepped away from me. "I'm going to go to the ladies' room." She set her teeth on her lower lip. "Just to clean up the best that I can."

I held in a growl at the thought of my cum dripping out of her. If we were somewhere more private, I would've pushed it back into her tight little hole.

After one more kiss to her forehead, I watched as she walked off to clean up in the bathroom.

And that was the last I saw of her.

It shouldn't have taken me so long to figure it out. She'd bolted after Jessica caught us red-handed in an awkward and compromising position with Irina on my desk, her legs spread wide. And it seemed that she'd bolted again.

I wanted to be mad, but deep down, I couldn't be. She wasn't running off because she wanted to put distance between us. I didn't think that was it. I suspected she was such a flight risk because she didn't know how else to act afterward.

I shouldn't have let her go.

I should've walked her there. Hell, I should've helped her clean up even if it was in the women's restroom in the library.

When it came to Irina, I was constantly caught up between what I should and shouldn't do. Now that I'd crossed a huge line of should and shouldn't with her, I couldn't care as much about being careful or walking delicately around her, as though she were forbidden.

For half of the next week, though, that wasn't an issue. She went into hiding again, or so it seemed. Her absence was noted at my English History class, and without her there, it just wasn't the same. I had no reason to be there, pretending I was lecturing without her there to listen. Without her being there for me to watch her expressions and wonder what she was thinking.

"She didn't come to the poetry class either," I told Rurik near the end of the week when I was curious whether he'd seen her.

"Maybe something is going on with Igor?"

His guess didn't fill me with any comforting hope. I was concerned about her, but I couldn't distinguish whether I felt like that because I wanted her again or if I anticipated something happening, like an attack from the Petrovs. My mind ran a mile a minute when I thought about her. That was how much more she'd gotten under my skin from just that one time we'd fucked in the library.

I took the initiative to try to follow her some more, checking in at the public places on campus where I'd seen her before. Going to her apartment seemed like the next best step, but I would save that as a last resort. Cameras would mark my presence there. While Irina was ignorant of who I was, someone watching the Petrov footage would be able to match me to whatever latest image someone might have on file of me somewhere. Like the Baranov organization, the Petrovs had access to hackers and expert IT servicers.

After I worked out one evening—another attempt to find her, in case she was there in that skin-tight gear while she did cardio—I got a call from one of the contacts I'd spoken with in Moscow.

"What the fuck?" I whispered to myself as I looked at the number, catching my breath from a run on the treadmill.

Of all people to call me, over a month since I'd left...

"Hello?"

"Hey, Vik," Timber answered. I never did get a solid explanation for what seemed like a cheesy, ridiculous nickname. Maybe it was an inside joke. It was irrelevant, but what he was calling to tell me wasn't. "I might have an update for you."

"Oh?" I'd been so focused on Irina and this current assignment that was a much-needed break from the whorehouses that I'd completely dismissed that cold case about Sonya. I, like so many others, had figured she was long gone. Dead.

"It looks like there's been activity in that account you were asking about."

I wiped my brow, stepping off the machine and leaving to have this call in private. "Really?" I had to wonder if the fact that I was recently in Moscow and asking around had triggered something to pop up or be revealed.

"Yeah. A withdrawal that couldn't be traced, but then almost the same amount put right back in."

"Hmm."

"I have a couple of guys looking into it, but like I said before, if anyone is behind this and it's not just a bunch of coincidences, this isn't the work of an amateur."

"I agree, Timber." The only leads that Oleg had ever received about the disappearance of Sonya and Boris's mother were loose trails of money that were hidden under layers of identities. Shell corps had him guessing for years who might have been behind the two women's disappearance—if anyone was behind it at all. Some, like Eva, believed that they'd just run away and hidden from the Baranov family, wanting out of the Mafia life and to be free like ordinary citizens.

Giving up on finishing this workout, I left and listened to the scant details Timber had to offer me. After I showered, I called Oleg to see if he wanted to meet up. I'd give him these updates as they came. That was only right.

He agreed to see me uptown, so I made the drive there. The further I got from the campus, the further from Irina, the more this longing and anxiousness settled in and took root. I couldn't be *this* smitten over her already. I couldn't be this desperate for the young virgin I'd fucked in the library. I wasn't some new lover, an idiot who would fall for the first pussy, the first woman who'd pay attention—

Whoa. Wait a second. Fall for?

"Forget about it," I muttered as I drove. I shook my head, amused by the way my thoughts were going. I was *not* falling for my target. I refused to admit that my feelings were getting too deep where the enemy was concerned.

"It's just sex." And I, more than many others, should be able to respect the difference between something like true intimacy and physical fucking. I'd immersed myself in the world of sex, managing whorehouses. My view of sex had been dulled. Yet, my opinions and nagging thoughts about Irina challenged me to wonder if I'd stumbled upon something different and something so real with her.

It's just because of the danger and mystery attached to all of this. If she were just a random twentysomething wandering into the whorehouse, I wouldn't have paid any extra attention to her.

I winced as I parked, hating the sensation that I was lying to myself.

Right?

Shelving my thoughts about Irina, I went into the warehouse where Oleg was supervising a couple of men torturing a Cartel member who'd been caught snooping around our warehouse, planting listening devices. In an office on an upper level, with one-way mirrored windows so we could look out at what happened down below, I faced the Boss.

He listened, always attentive and sharp, as I updated him about this fresh call from Timber.

"In other words," he summed up without any strong emotion, suggesting he was tired of the lack of answers, "nothing new."

"Sounds like it." I shrugged and put my hands in my pockets.

"Thank you for updating me."

"No problem." While it would've made more sense for Timber to just contact Oleg himself, we maintained my role as a middle man to insulate both sides. Not just anyone could call or speak with Oleg Baranov. He was too powerful to be that accessible.

"I'm glad you had a chance to drive in and speak with me," he added, giving me a curious look. "Not too busy following the Petrov girl today?"

I shook my head. There was no way in hell I would tell him that I *had* followed her recently, like in the library before I gagged her and fucked her. "She's been lying low lately."

"I'm not surprised."

I furrowed my brow, instantly alert for what *he* could know.

"I was curious about what you said about that night when the Ilyin men were trying to capture her at that gathering." He stared at me, serious and pensive. "So curious that I asked around about any chance the Ilyins might want to cause a diversion for Igor Petrov."

I nodded. "I considered that as well."

"Or if they wanted to provoke him by taking his only daughter."

Again, I nodded in agreement. Those thoughts had hit me as well.

"What I heard is more surprising, though." He cleared his throat then continued in his raspy smoker's voice that wasn't helped by his love of cigars. "It sounds like Igor Petrov is promising Irina in marriage to one of the Ilyins. Andre Ilyin, perhaps."

I'd seen that fucker on campus, too. He had to be watching her, maybe motivated to do so because he thought he'd be marrying her.

I tensed, immediately loathing the possibility of Irina being married to… well, anyone. I'd claimed her virginity. She'd shown interest in me. The thought of her with any other man filled me with rage.

"Any thoughts on that?" Oleg asked, not judging, not fishing for anything.

I must have gone silent for longer than I'd realized. Fuming and trying to accept the gravity of this news, I blinked and searched for a response.

I had too many thoughts about Irina being promised in marriage to anyone. I couldn't handle the image of another man even touching her. Being this possessive over her was another *shouldn't* when it came to my rights with her, but I couldn't help it.

She's mine.

My target. My enemy. My obsession. Irina Petrov was too damn perfect for me to envision her belonging with anyone else.

I furrowed my brow, knowing I had to give him an answer, one that wouldn't lower his faith or respect for me after an admission that I'd slept with the enemy. He wouldn't be bothered if I'd slept with her for the sake of seducing her and manipulating her for intel, but he wouldn't be on board with my wanting more intimacy with her for the sake of feeling complete.

"Do you trust that word?" I hated how defensive and combative I sounded. "Do you believe that he would arrange for her to marry one of them?"

He pursed his lips. "Marrying his daughter into the family of his enemy?" He shrugged. "It happens. It has happened, but it is usually in the case of surrender. Or a ploy for something else to be gained in the transaction."

His words lingered on my mind long after I left. During the drive back to my apartment, I acted on this new urgency to make sure that couldn't happen.

Irina would not marry a fucking Ilyin. She couldn't be displaced from *me*.

Calling Rurik was my first step. But he wasn't convinced my plan was wise.

"You want me to distract the Petrov guards from her so you can do *what?*" he asked.

"Get her guards away from her so I can take her." I hadn't stuttered.

"Take her… to question her?"

"No. Just to have her. I—" While I knew better than to open my mouth to Oleg and say that I wanted her, I wasn't as guarded with Rurik, with a brother. "I want her secure away from the influence of her father's men."

"Okay…" He still didn't sound convinced.

It was past time for me to ask her about what Igor Petrov was up to. I had to be more direct. No more Professor Remi seducing his naughty student. It was time for me to be Vik, the lover who didn't want her to be given to someone else, the man who was daring to hope she couldn't be stuck on the side of the enemy forever.

I couldn't dismiss her as *only* the enemy. Not when she helped Eva escape. Not when she had yet to act like she was committed to her father or family.

Because I couldn't stand the thought of her with someone else, I had to get her somewhere I could ask her the hard questions and get to the bottom of what her father was planning—with or without her help.

As soon as Rurik got her guards away, I'd track her down and get down to all these questions she owed me answers for.

20

IRINA

Early the next morning, I set out to work for my father. The last couple of days, I fell down one rabbit hole after another. When I wasn't researching how to start over with a new identity for myself and Maxim, I was putting some effort into looking into Marcus James and Eric Benson. Both of the up-and-coming politicians were sexy and photogenic, which probably helped them get as far as they had, at least via social media. No one liked an ugly politician, after all.

Missing classes, staying in, and just poring over what I found on my laptop, I kept myself safe. Safe from being exposed and vulnerable to a frisky Ilyin trying to capture me again because my father wanted to play games with them.

I also needed to retreat and stay safe from Viktor, too. After he took me so hard and fast in the library, I wanted it again. I wanted *him* again, not just for how well he'd fucked me, so filthily and taboo like that, but because he'd given a damn and asked me what I wanted. No one ever had, and that was a dangerous thing to get used to.

I couldn't get used to him. That was clear. He belonged here at school, teaching and seducing young women like me. Whereas I belonged... working for my father just so he wouldn't make Maxim suffer. Yesterday, he'd sent me a picture of canceling food deliveries to Maxim. The guard would be fed, but my brother would not. Unless I had something to tell him before tonight, he would cancel the incoming order.

So, I would do as he bade. From my snooping online, I found a few connections that I could start looking into. By checking out who liked what and who had friended whom, a network of acquaintances was clearer to see and follow.

Before I would need to go to Viktor's class, I left my apartment to follow a student who was a well-known dealer on campus. I'd noticed him talking with Ilyin men who came here now and then, but that affiliation wasn't anything new. I'd already identified him and reported him to my father as a connection of some kind.

What I wanted to investigate now was why he was commenting about talking to a student worker in the dean's office. Marcus James had also made a comment elsewhere, and I deduced that the three of them might be planning a meeting or rendezvous point.

Either way, it was a connection I had to follow—if for no other reason than to prove to Igor that I was doing my duty here. I'd be damned if Maxim was starved because of what our father deemed as my slacking off.

I walked into the building where the dean's office was located. Multiple offices were housed in here, a collective grouping of dean's officials who carried out many administrative tasks. Pretending to scroll on my phone, I meandered down the hallways until I could locate that student worker. Wherever he was, he'd sure picked a good hiding spot to talk to a dealer and Marcus. I couldn't find them anywhere, and that was saying something since not many office workers were in this early.

I did find one person, though, and it wasn't anyone I wanted to see anytime soon. Twice, I'd caught sight of Jessica Nolan near Viktor. She was obviously interested in him, and that was all I knew about her. As she stalked up to me in the hallway, pausing my plan to snoop and find a meeting to listen in on, I got the feeling she was about to show me how vindictive and catty she could be.

"What are you doing here?" She narrowed her eyes at me.

I shrugged. "Looking for someone."

"The offices aren't open yet."

I nodded. "Okay. Sorry."

Before she would let me walk away, she had to slip in the last word. In this case, a threat.

"I know what you're doing."

Oh, shit. She must have been watching me snoop longer than I realized.

"You're just another slut eager for a good grade. Fucking your professor…" Her lip curled in disdain.

Oh! That was all? She was a sore loser about how I'd gotten Viktor. She wasn't putting me on the spot for snooping. *Whew.*

"I'm not," I argued.

She took one step toward, and I reacted by getting into a defensive stance, just in case she'd make this physical.

"I know what I saw."

In his office, she did. Or she could guess. We'd been mostly covered up, springing apart when she opened the door. Viktor and I hadn't had sex there. We had in the library, but no one saw us.

I think.

"I will ruin you, bitch." She pointed at me, getting in my face. "I will ruin you for taking a man I had my eye on."

I shook my head, furious that someone else other than my father was trying to make my life even more difficult. Ignoring her, I turned and gave her my back. Engaging in that conversation wouldn't help anything. She wouldn't listen to me. And I refused to listen to her.

She didn't pursue me as I walked away, but I felt the burn of her stare on my back.

"Fuck you," I mumbled as I headed to Viktor's lecture. "You can just fuck off and leave me alone."

Jessica Nolan would have to take a number and get in line if she wanted to join the forces against me.

I took a seat toward the front of Viktor's class, letting all my other worries fall to the back of my mind as I watched him enter. Just like every other lecture he gave, he spoke dryly, almost as if *he* was bored about the material too.

In a sharp suit, his signature bold-red tie, and a no-nonsense expression of wanting to get this business done, he droned on. I hardly listened, too mesmerized by the sight of him. With amazement and wonder filling my head, I tried to believe that this sexy man had really fucked me like I wanted him to. That he'd used a tie just like the one he was wearing to gag me and keep me quiet while he rammed his big dick into my virgin body.

Just thinking back to that night had me aroused all over again. It seemed that avoiding him for two days hadn't done a damn thing toward reducing the impact he had on me.

I wasn't only staring at him with sex on my mind, though. With his grumpy, gruff voice and furrowed brow, he looked mad. Or annoyed.

Is he irritated, seeing me after I avoided him?

Does he regret having sex with me?

After class, it seemed I would have an answer. He approached me, heading directly toward me as students filed out.

"Come to my office and see me about your grade." It wasn't an invitation. It was an order.

I licked my lower lip and nodded. "Sure."

I guess that means he doesn't want to be done with me yet...

I gathered my things and went to his office. He wasn't there yet, wrapping up his things from the lecture. When he showed up, striding confidently down the hall, I had to hold my breath and not let a needy noise slip free. He couldn't know how damn fine he was, how sexy he was, tall, strong, and so sure of himself.

Looking me directly in the eye but not saying a word, he unlocked his door and gestured for me to enter.

As soon as I walked in and he joined me there, he shut the door behind me and pushed me up against it.

His hard mouth slanted down over mine, and I didn't need baby steps into this kiss. Pushing up against him as I wrapped my arms around his neck, I gasped and tried to keep up with the desire burning between us, both of us always so attuned to needing the other with a fierce impatience.

I moaned into his mouth, twirling my tongue around his then sucking on it. A deep growl rumbled from his chest as he snaked his arms around me, still forcing me back to the door.

Making out with him thrilled me. Already, I was getting wet for him, eager to feel his dick deep inside me again, his fingers on my breasts. All of him. I wanted to rip off my clothes and beg him to show me himself, too.

But he wasn't on the same page. Backing up without actually releasing me, he panted and shook his head.

I lowered my hand to cup the bulge of his erection in his pants.

"No," he rasped. "Not here. Not now."

"But—"

He kissed me hard, brutal and demanding in that hot touch. "No. Not like this." Stepping back completely, he ran his hand through his blond hair and gave me such a smoldering once-over that I wondered how my clothes hadn't fallen off yet. "I can't trust that Jessica wouldn't barge in here again."

I rolled my eyes, not ready to be told no. "You can lock the door."

"And she could unlock it. I caught her snooping in here yesterday. And I always keep that door locked when I'm not here."

I pouted, sagging against the door. I'd been interested in talking to him, though, to figure out why he seemed so mad during the lecture, so I supposed I could ignore this raging need for him for a little while.

"I'll pick you up at eight," he said matter-of-factly as he adjusted his erection beneath his pants. "Fuck, it'll kill me to wait that long."

I laughed lightly, almost incredulously. It was almost surreal to think that he and I were doing this, whatever I could technically call this sleeping-with-your-hot-professor thing.

"You will, huh?"

He grinned, looking at me like he wanted to fuck me now. "Yes. Be ready for me at eight."

If he kept staring at me like he wanted to ruin me for any other man on this planet, I wasn't sure if I'd ever be ready for him.

But there was no chance in hell I was backing out and missing this opportunity to be with him, no matter where it would take me. "Eight," I confirmed, already excited.

21

VIKTOR

Tonight would be the night. I'd get her away from the campus. I'd remove her from her guards' reach. And I would ask her what Igor Petrov was plotting.

It would also be the night where I could have my way with her. Taking her virginity in the library was hot. It was fast and dirty, but it was far from what I wanted. I needed to see her, to feel every soft inch of her. I wanted to show her all of me and watch her suck my cock. This time, I could savor every minute of her without any distractions or interruptions.

I pulled up to her apartment building five minutes before eight, pleased that she walked right out to my car. She was ready, on time, and perhaps excited to spend time with me judging by how eager she was for my arrival.

Admiring her confident stride as she walked through the snow toward my car, I groaned and wondered how I would be able to refrain from fucking her tonight. I'd have to hold off until I got my answers. But it wouldn't be easy to torture myself with her so near.

After she got in the car, she glanced at me and almost smiled. "Hi."

"Hi." Since the windows were tinted, I leaned over, cupped her chin, and pulled her over the center console so I could kiss her. She sighed, not opening her eyes yet afterward, as if she wanted to treasure the kiss.

"Where are your… friends?" I asked.

"Hmm?" She buckled in as I put the car into drive.

"Your guards."

She paused for a beat before speaking again. "Guards?"

I nodded. I couldn't give it away that I recognized the two men near her as Petrov soldiers. I had to keep her in the dark about who I really was for a while longer. But I could inquire as any other person might have. "Your bodyguards?"

She released a long exhale. "Yes, my guards. They, um, were sent to handle something else."

"How come you have them?" I asked, keeping my tone light and casual, not businesslike or demanding.

"I come from a very influential family. My father's line of work requires that I have a security detail."

I nodded, pretending to absorb this news. "Then how come they weren't at that party when I protected you from those men trying to kidnap you?"

"They didn't think it would be a dangerous event for me to go to." She shrugged, looking out the side window.

Yeah, I'm not sure I'm buying that. If Igor wanted guards on his daughter when she was on campus and behaving like a college student, why wouldn't they follow her to a party in a shitty and dangerous part of town? Something wasn't adding up.

I held off on asking any more questions for now. Before I could take her to my place—the penthouse I called home, not my apartment I was using near the campus—I had to stop at one of the whorehouses and pick up a package. It wasn't something I wanted to deal with, but sometimes these kinds of favors were expected. I'd drop off the package to another Baranov boss tomorrow, but it would be better if this package of currency wasn't at the whorehouse all night, vulnerable to be stolen.

"I just need to make a stop first."

She laughed lightly. "You haven't even told me where you're taking me."

"Yet you agreed anyway."

The look she gave me was a sweet one. "I trust you, Viktor."

Fuck me. She was killing me with this easy submission. She couldn't be any more perfect.

"Should I trust *you*?" I asked as I parked outside.

She glanced around the building, furrowing her brow and seeming confused. "I think you can."

Interesting answer, enemy of mine.

"It depends," she added.

Aha.

"Can I trust you to come inside with me for a moment and agree not to tell anyone about what you see?"

She nodded, either used to being expected to keep secrets or scared to tell me no.

I helped her out of the car and led her inside. The music, the sounds of sex, the *smell* of sex. She had to be overwhelmed by it all. Yet, her fingers didn't tremble within my grip. She didn't gawk or flinch as I walked her further into the whorehouse.

The Baranov Family had just as many sex clubs as they did whorehouses, but one thing stayed the same between them—surveillance

LEONA WHITE

and security. Every room in this brothel had a camera so we could collect evidence, gather blackmail, and generally cover our asses.

In what was called the command center, I grabbed the package I was supposed to deliver tomorrow. On three walls of the room, monitors showed the various states of activities happening in all the rooms. Letting Irina stand in the middle, staring wide-eyed at all the screens, I stepped aside to check with the man on duty.

Then I returned to her, hugging her from behind. "See anything you like?" I whispered as I kissed below her neck.

"What…" She swallowed hard. "What is this?"

"What does it look like?"

She couldn't tear her gaze away from the screen with the man spanking a woman as he fucked her from behind.

"It looks like… nothing I would ever expect from an English professor."

I chuckled darkly, nuzzling her neck and kissing her sweet flesh. "I never said that was the *only* job I've ever had." Running my hand over her stomach, I hugged her closer and pushed her back into me.

"I have so many questions," she muttered, staring at the scenes on the monitors.

Me too.

"Then let's get out of here and you can ask them."

She turned her head to peer at me. "Would you answer them?"

I nodded. "What do you want to know first?"

"If you'd do that to me." She looked again at the screen that had captured her attention the most.

I grinned, taking her hand and leading her out of the room. I didn't let go of her hand all through the lobby I brought her through, passing the clientele and whores who were waiting for a room. I reclaimed her hand in the car as I drove her to my place. Up the elevator ride, I maintained my grip on her fingers as if I feared letting go of her would make me lose her forever. She was a goddamn dream, one I hadn't realized I'd been waiting for.

But the second we were in my penthouse, I used my hold on her hand to spin her and bring her down on the nearest sofa. She landed over my lap, squeaking in surprise. Before she could finish that startled reaction, I lifted her skirt and smacked my hand on her sweet cheek, reddening her ass.

"Ah!" She cried out at the strike, squirming.

I growled, mesmerized by the sight of her bare cheek, pink from my handprint. "You naughty, *naughty* girl…"

She wasn't wearing anything. Not a thong. No panties.

"Did you forget to put something on?" I asked as I stroked my finger down her crack until I found her pussy.

She moaned, lowering her head until she rested her cheek on my thigh. Her legs parted, giving me access to finger her. Already, she was so slick and wet. "I didn't forget," she replied saucily.

I spanked her again, rewarded with more of her juices coating my fingers.

"You deliberately met me with nothing on under your skirt?"

She nodded. "Why bother? You rip my panties, anyway."

"You naughty little thing." I rained my hand down twice more, rubbing her perfect, round globes as she moaned and writhed.

I was supposed to be questioning her. She made it sound like she looked forward to a conversation with me, too. But now that we'd started down this path…

I can't wait.

Shifting her further off my lap but within reach so I could continue to finger her, I encouraged her to get up on her hands and knees.

"Unzip me," I ordered as I spread my legs apart a bit.

With her to my right, on all fours as she hurried to undo my pants, I slid two fingers in and out of her juicy cunt. When she reached her hand in to pull my hard cock out, I spanked her.

"Did I tell you to do that?"

She lowered, moaning at the spank.

"Use your mouth," I instructed.

As she lowered her head to put her lips around my cock, I growled and added another finger, stretching her. With her sexy mouth, she sucked me and maneuvered so my dick was standing up for her to play with. She didn't need any more guidance from me on how to suck me off. While I could tell she was an amateur, probably never having done this before based on her jerky, inexperienced moves, she was eager to please me.

I let her learn, to find what she liked, and within minutes, I doubted I could last.

"Stop," I ordered with another spank. She moaned, humming around my cock stuffed in her mouth.

She pulled up and looked at me, pleading. "I don't want to."

I growled, forcing her head back down on my dick as I thrust my hips up to fuck her mouth. "No, you don't want to do as you're told?" I pulled my fingers out of her cunt to spank her harder.

She sucked harder.

"Fuck, sweetheart." I couldn't stop pumping my hips, driving my dick up into her warm mouth. Fingering her again, stretching her, I fought not to shoot my load down her throat. "You want me to come in your mouth? Or in this tight little pussy?"

She moaned again, still licking and sucking me off.

"Answer me!" I spanked her again.

This time, on the pull up, she gasped and let out a cry of relief.

Unwilling to miss her coming, I slid my fingers back into her and pistoned them, prolonging her orgasm as I flipped her onto the couch. Still dressed, I climbed over her and replaced my fingers with my cock. She trembled, arching her back as I slammed in fast.

"Vik!" She couldn't find the strength to finish my name, so lost to coming hard.

Determined to make sure I gave her what she wanted, to make her live out what she saw at the brothel, I pulled out, staggered to stand, then flipped her so she bent over the couch. Pounding into her pussy again, I spanked her ass until she came again. Squeezing me so tight, she triggered me to follow her. I rained my palm on her reddened cheek one more time as I used my other hand to pull her waist back to me.

"Just like that, sweetheart. Fuck. Just like that," I groaned.

Flooding her womb with my cum, I realized it was no longer a matter of wanting to give her what she wanted. It was a marathon of proving to myself that she was all I would ever want. Now and forever.

22

IRINA

I didn't know what I was agreeing to when Viktor told me that he'd pick me up at eight. There wasn't any chance I would've told him no.

Now that I was waking next to him in bed the morning after he got me from my apartment, I never wanted to leave.

He fucked me so hard and rough on the couch, spanking my ass until it burned. It was so bad, wrong to want him at all, wrong of me to be so thrilled that my professor was spanking my ass. Knowing how inappropriate it was made it all the hotter.

I'd barely come down from the high of coming on the couch before he moved us. Dizzy and lost to such a powerful orgasm, I was disoriented and floating on bliss when he carried me into a huge shower, an enormous stall that rivaled the size of what could be found at my father's house. As he washed us, taking care to caress my red ass and treating me to both a shower and a massage, I lost track of noticing all the details about his bathroom.

Then, as the shower turned into more foreplay, he brought me to his king-sized bed and made love to me there. It felt presumptuous to think that—making love. But that was what it was like. Not as hard and rough, which I did like, but slow, gentle, and tender. If he wasn't on a mission to show me how varied of a lover he could be, he was proving it, anyway. Fast or slow. Hard or soft. No matter how he was when he put his hands and mouth on me, his cock inside me, he showed me how treasured a woman could feel.

He woke next to me, moaning in a sexy, sleepy manner that made me smile. Stretching while he was still flush to me, he rubbed his hard, muscled, hot body alongside mine.

"Hi," I said, hating how lame I sounded.

He was amused, smiling slowly and pulling me in for a deep kiss. "Hi," he whispered back. "Don't tell me you have a class you need to get to."

I laughed. "It's Saturday," I reminded him.

"Oh. Good."

"Am I interfering with your weekend plans?" I asked. I hadn't counted on spending the night. Peter and the other guard were busy doing something else for my father. I doubted anyone would notice my leaving my apartment last night via the cameras. Because I didn't matter to them. I was just a burden.

"No. But you're helping me make some." With that, he slid me closer to him. As he spooned me, he picked up my thigh and draped it back over his so he could stroke his fingers over my slit.

"You're insatiable," I teased.

"For you, sweetheart. The things that you make me want to do…" He growled, kissing the side of my neck as he played with me.

"Tell me." I pushed my ass back toward him. "Please?"

"You make me want to fuck you until you can't stand." He pushed his fingers a little further, lightly penetrating but keeping his touch so light that it was a tease.

LEONA WHITE

"I'd say you're halfway there." Talking about sex got me wondering about where he'd taken me last night. And now that I was awake, I noticed how well furnished his bedroom was. Viktor had commented that being a professor wasn't his only job. But at the moment when he said that, I couldn't tell if he meant his only job currently or ever. He was clearly loaded.

As we lay there, his finger stroking and his lips pressing under my ear, I thought back to all the things that didn't quite make sense.

"You're thinking too much," he said, dipping his finger deeper into me.

"If you keep that up, I won't."

He went still, and I groaned. "No, please. Don't stop."

He resumed his touch, but too lightly and slowly to get me off. "I want to know. What's on your mind?"

I laughed lightly. "Are you pretending that I'm not just a piece of ass to you?"

"You're not." He turned me slightly until I faced him, his finger still hooked in place inside me. "I want to know you. Inside and out. You're more than just an easy lay, sweetheart." After placing a tender kiss to my brow as he moved his finger again, he lay back down and spooned me again. "I want to know what you're thinking."

"I was thinking that not everything adds up about you."

"Like what?" He followed his question by kissing me.

"Like your taking me to that…" I furrowed my brow, impatient when he didn't keep up with his fingers sliding in and out. "Where was that place?"

"A whorehouse," he answered simply.

That was my best guess. I'd been so shocked by it all that I hadn't asked.

"So, you're just an average college professor who frequents whorehouses?"

"I've never visited them as a guest."

That makes less sense.

"And a professor who's loaded?" I moaned as he leaned lower to suck my nipple. "This place is… fancy."

"I have money," he confirmed.

"But not from being a professor?"

He shook his head. "Other things."

I couldn't help but feel like there were two sides to this hunk of man who could make me feel so good. I was only meeting one half, though. "Vik?"

"Hmmm?" He moved his thumb to my clit, and I arched into his touch.

"A big part of why I want you is because you're so different from the men I've met so far. The men I have met through my father's business. I like that you're such a 'normal' guy, a stranger who can meet me and form independent opinions about me. And you want me."

"Of course, I do."

Still, he wouldn't comment on what I said. He wasn't filling in the gaps.

"I can't imagine why. What a professor could hope to do with one of his students. What kind of a future you are looking for."

He teased me still, stroking me, fingering me, and playing dirty by increasing his attention on my clit. "I can see a future with you. In my bed. Making me hard." Moving me away, he shifted so he could sit up. He held his long, thick shaft, stroking himself as he watched me. "Telling you how much I love it when you suck me."

I smiled, slightly irked that he was distracting me with sex. It was too tempting to resist, though. I wasn't sure I could prove that I knew what I was doing, but I hoped I made up for my inexperience with enthusiasm.

Crawling over, I lowered my mouth to his dick. First I licked the tip, then I circled my tongue around the wide head.

As I explored and sucked him, he encouraged me to move up the bed while he reclined. Once he pushed me over him, so he could align his face with my pussy, he decided to talk again.

"I've never really considered my future too much," he admitted in between kisses he placed up the insides of my thighs while he stroked his finger in me.

I had never done something like this, and the naughtiness of it was exhilarating.

"But I've always wondered if and when I'd find a woman who'd make sense in my life."

I smiled, slowing my sucks on his big dick. "Me?" I ventured to guess, kissing along his wet shaft.

He pulled my hips lower so he could nuzzle at my entrance, kissing and sucking hard. As he pushed me back up and thrust his dick at my mouth, he replied, "No."

I pouted as I sucked on him again, bothered by his answer and the fact that he'd slowed down on me.

"Nothing about you makes sense, Irina. We shouldn't be together for many reasons."

I lifted off him. "Why?"

"Keep that mouth busy," he ordered. As soon as I complied with his bossiness, he moved me closer so he could lick all my cream. After he replaced his mouth with his finger, he continued, "Because you're supposed to be my student while I'm your professor."

Supposed to be? How am I not?

"Because you're sixteen years younger than me."

How does he know my age?

"And because our backgrounds are… different."

He could say that again. I would never relate to him, stuck as a Mafia princess and expected to do as my father decided.

"Despite all that," he said, "I'm starting to convince myself that I can fight to keep you."

I sucked harder, somehow turned on that much more at his devoted words.

"That you and I could figure out how to be together."

I hummed my approval.

"That's the future that I want to make my reality, sweetheart. I want to keep you. All to myself."

Moved by his words and wishing they could come true, I doubled down to please him, as if it could be a token of gratitude that he'd want me so badly after knowing me for such a short time—knowing the version of myself that I let him know.

He stopped talking, adjusting me so I straddled his face. I sucked on him while he ate at me. Before long, under his encouragement, I ground down on his face. He looped his arms up to grab my ass and secure me over him. The closer I came to my orgasm that remained just out of reach, I worried how I would breathe around him. Taking my mouth off him wasn't happening. I was determined to please him, to show him how much I wanted him too. I was no expert, not like any of those whores in that house. I was naïve but eager to prove my worth.

Fighting back the pleasure of his mouth under me, I breathed through my nose and hummed at the satisfaction of his finally coming. Jerking up into me, he emptied himself in my mouth. Jet after jet of hot, salty cum shot into my throat.

He growled, digging his fingers into my ass as he nipped the sucked at me, pushing me to come with him.

Just finished with swallowing down every last drop, I wrenched up as my release hit me. I ground down on his face as I leaned on my arms, locking my elbows. As the waves of pleasure rocketed through me, dizzying me, I humped him and sought every last morsel of friction he could give me.

It wasn't easy to believe him when he said this wasn't just sex between us. It felt like it was. Yet, as he carried me into the shower to clean up again moments later, I snuggled into his hold and realized how sweet it would be to rely on his vision of a future together. In bed and out of it.

It wasn't the future I knew I could have. One day soon, someday soon, I would kill my father and have to run with Maxim. That had been the ultimate goal for so long.

I hadn't counted on meeting a man who could entice me to want something else, something more.

In the shower again, held within his strong embrace, I battled back the angst of still never being able to have what I wanted.

I wanted him.

And I wanted freedom from my father.

Those endings could happen at the same time and overlap, though, so with a heavy heart, I vowed to enjoy every second with Viktor that I could while it lasted.

23

VIKTOR

Maybe I fucked her too hard. Irina went quiet after I introduced her to the art of sixty-nine.

It was a pleasant surprise when I woke up and found her still there. With her track record, I wouldn't have been off the mark to assume she'd run again. She stayed, though, the whole night and the morning after. And seeing her in my space made it so easy for me to seriously imagine her staying in my life. For good.

I'd come close to telling her the truth. I knew she was suspicious of me and what she didn't know about me. She was sharp, realizing that I didn't represent the lifestyle of a standard professor.

But I couldn't bring myself to tell her the truth. Not when I was certain I was well on my way to falling for her.

When I described how different we were, evading any details that she could pick up on that would clue her in to the fact that I knew all about who she was, I heard the pang of sadness in her voice when she replied.

That she was so drawn to me because she perceived me to be someone outside her world. She saw me as Professor Viktor Remi, a "normal" man. And the distinct contrast to the Mafia men she was used to was a pro, not a con.

Yet, I was as Mafia as Mafia could get. I was Vik Baranov, behind-the-scenes soldier and leader who supervised whorehouses.

If she knew that I wasn't who she thought I was, if she learned how similar—yet apart—I was to the life she knew, a Mafia man from a rival Family, I would lose her. I'd sever that connection that she liked, this idea that a so-called normal man could want someone like her. It was a complex of hidden and altered identities, and I worried that it would ruin what we were building.

Because after I dropped her off, I knew I would fight for us. There had to be a way to bring her to my side. I had to figure out how to wrench her out of Igor Petrov's influence and firmly convert her into being a Baranov. With me.

I'd distracted her with sex all night and morning. It prevented me from asking her what her father was up to. If I wanted to prolong the secret of who I was for a little longer, I couldn't ask her about Igor.

It might have seemed like I was being stupid, foolish for a woman, but I had enough sense to detect hints that she might not be loyal to Igor. The way that she had secretly helped Eva and Lev escape stood for something. It stood for a lot. That action was dangerous and altruistic, putting herself at risk of her family's anger just to help a rival.

She can't be loyal to him.

Yet, I refused to let myself completely believe that because I feared I was already too prejudiced in wanting her to be loyal to only *me*.

Talking to Eva and Lev would help. Even Rurik. They could help shed light on what might be going on. I could only hope it wouldn't take too long. If the Ilyins thought that Irina would be promised to them, a ticking time bomb was working against me now.

Sunday, I focused all my efforts on looking for answers about Igor's plans without involving Irina. She couldn't be the only source of intel.

I followed the one burly guard, Peter. I hung out near a few Ilyins at a bar off campus. I listened in on a couple of Petrov soldiers who seemed to be waiting for a man in a suit to meet them near the dean's office.

By the time night fell, I had learned a whole bunch of nothing. Frustrated and worrying that I was putting myself up to an impossible challenge, I slept restlessly and woke up annoyed at the world. After starting my morning with Irina next to me, naked and warm and inviting, I didn't want to start my days any other way.

I got coffee and walked through the snowless but frigid weather toward the lecture hall. At least I'd be able to see her there and not have to settle for sexting like she had yesterday.

I reached the double doors to the building, frowning when Rurik pushed off the wall he'd been standing at. He approached me quickly, his brow furrowed and eyes serious.

"What's wrong?" I asked. There was no point asking *if* something was wrong.

"Everyone knows." He fell into step with me, entering the building.

Heat blasted at my face from the overhead furnace, almost burning my eyes. "Everyone knows what?"

"About you and Irina." He looked around, ever cautious that someone could be listening. After he tugged his beanie off his head, he pushed his hair back to glance at me. "That you've claimed her."

"Everyone, as in people here at the college? Or...?"

"Everyone in *our* world, Vik. What the fuck were you thinking?"

I stopped, glaring at him. "Don't pretend that you didn't know I was going to seduce her to get her to open up to me and talk."

Which... I haven't actually done yet.

"Yeah. Seduce her. As in tease her and maybe get her off. One night or something. Not take her home. To your *real* home."

I frowned, missing too many dots to connect. I had been contemplating talking to him about how I was developing serious feelings for her, but I hadn't said a single thing. How could he be aware that I hadn't seduced her but instead fell for her?

"How do you know..." I shook my head, needing to back this up. "*What* do you know?"

"Everyone's talking about how you claimed Igor's only daughter. Everyone in all the Families around here know that you stole the bride Petrov told the Ilyins that they could have."

"We don't know that Igor did promise her to anyone. Oleg told me that he was thinking it was a prank or only a rumor."

He shrugged. "The Ilyins seem to think it was a legitimate arrangement. They're pissed. I just found out this morning, listening in to a couple of lines I tapped, and I wanted to inform you as soon as possible."

I scoffed. "What? You think the Ilyins are going to come after me now?"

"I don't see why they wouldn't now."

I narrowed my eyes, scanning the hallway. The doors to the lecture hall were right there. I was due to start class in a minute. I'd see Irina in there. But Rurik seemed to think I had to worry about my life, not that my cover could be blown.

I felt lousy. If what Rurik said was true, word could reach Irina. And I'd just had this weekend to come clean and really talk to her, to expose myself in order to ask her what Igor was up to. But I hadn't. Guilt hit me that I hadn't been open and taken a risk on how she felt about me, that she could genuinely feel about me to the same depth that I did about her.

Confused, I tried to understand how I'd gotten to this point. "How did word get out that I was with her at all?" We hadn't done anything publicly. Jessica had interrupted us in my office, but she wasn't affiliated with anyone in the Mafia to spread word.

"Someone saw you at the whorehouse. With her."

"Fuck." I ran my hand down my face, more pissed at myself than anything else. I'd taken her in the back way to collect that package I had to deliver, which I did. When I saw how excited she looked from watching the monitors, though, I didn't pay attention to leaving the way we'd entered. I'd held her hand as I walked her through the foyer of the whorehouse. And anyone in the city could've been there waiting to get in a room. Even a soldier from a rival family.

"Fuck!" I repeated before grinding my teeth hard.

"Yeah, fuck is right," he agreed, so worried as he watched me nearly explode with anger. "The only silver lining is that no one seems to know you're, well, you."

I stared at him expectantly, waiting for him to elaborate.

"No one seems to realize you're a Baranov. Just a man from here."

Nodding, I tried to calm down with that news. That was good. That helped. Because if Igor or the Ilyins knew a rival family member had interfered with a potential arranged engagement, I'd be well and truly fucked. Oleg would hear about it. And I would most definitely have a target on my back.

"Do you think..." I winced, unable to finish my question.

"What?" Rurik asked as the last students in the hall shuffled into the lecture room for the class I was supposed to start in seconds.

"Does Igor know?"

He nodded. "I assume. Gossip spreads that fast, man."

The fucker could hurt her for this. He could retaliate on *her*.

"I'll handle this."

The only plan that formed in my mind was reaching her and protecting her from any fallout from our getting together like we had.

"Let me help," he insisted. "I'm here to help."

I nodded, shuffling to the side to hurry into the big room where she should be waiting for class to start. "I'll get ahold of you. I have to get to her first."

Leaving Rurik in the hallway, I strode into the cavernous auditorium. My dress shoes clacked on the floor with my fast gait, and the sound echoed. No one spoke. I'd trained them that well to shut the fuck up so I could do my thing.

The second I reached the podium, I scanned the sea of faces peering at me. Methodically roving my gaze over row after row of students waiting for me to start this lecture, I fought the panic that rose inside me.

She's not here.

Irina's face wasn't in the crowd.

She hadn't come to class.

When she missed it before or showed up late, I was curious and worried. Today, after what Rurik said, I was downright concerned.

Scared, even.

Without any preamble, I cleared my throat then announced, "Class is canceled." I didn't wait for a reaction. I didn't linger to offer an explanation or reason. Before the mob of students could delay me in getting out of here, I turned on my heel and left.

I have to find her. Now.

I could only hope I wasn't too late.

24

IRINA

The last time I slept for more than six hours was when I had the flu a couple of years ago.

My body had been so exhausted that I didn't get out of bed for three days.

The Sunday after I spent the night at Viktor's penthouse, I slept. And slept. And slept some more. I wasn't ill. But I had been exhausted after how he'd kept me up and made sure I didn't go for long without his filling me and pushing me to come. Over and over. It was a glorious reason to need to catch up on sleep, and I wished against wishes that his idea of a perfect future could come true.

A life with Viktor would be heaven, but it wasn't meant to be.

He wouldn't be able to stand up to my father. One sexy professor wouldn't be a foe for a crime boss hell-bent on being the top leader in the area.

Besides, if I wanted to be selfish and start a life with Viktor, I would have to give up Maxim. I couldn't protect him if I no longer served Igor.

I woke early on Monday, wondering how Viktor would act with me in his class after having me in his bed. The reason I got up earlier than usual wasn't because of my alarms going off but because Peter and another guard knocked and entered my apartment.

They never let themselves in like that. My curiosity was piqued, to say the least. I dressed quickly and exited my room. "What's going on?"

Both of them glared at me like I was the worst excuse for a job in the universe.

"The Boss wants to see you."

Boss. Never Father. I rolled my eyes. "Now what?"

"Lose the attitude," Peter growled.

The brightness I woke up with faded. I wondered what His Highness was mad about now, but I didn't try to make conversation on the ride there.

We arrived, and I got out of the backseat quickly, wondering if this would take long or if I'd make it to Viktor's class on time.

My father was pacing in the study, furious and impatient. Veins bulged near his temple, and with a streak of darkness, I wondered with glee if he'd stroke right now. He couldn't have very good blood pressure with his diet and lack of exercise.

"What is it?" I asked, careful not to put any sass or attitude into my "greeting." Cutting to the chase would be nice, though.

"Don't fucking talk to me like that," he roared. "All the shit I do for you, and this is how you repay me?" He lifted his arm to backhand me, but I raised my arms to deflect him. He may be fat and old and taller, but I was by far more fit and quicker.

"What is your problem?" I asked, already sick of him after being in his presence for ten seconds.

"My problem is you think going to college means you can run around and be a fucking slut!" He paced away then came back, more furious. "My problem is you think being out of this house for two minutes gives you the right to act like a goddamn whore!"

I tensed, bracing for a hit. His words were a direct strike. I didn't know how he could even begin to think that I was acting like a slut or a whore. I wasn't. But since I'd recently lost my virginity to Viktor and spent the night at his place, it wasn't far-fetched to assume he knew about it somehow. He was aware of what I'd been up to. To an extent. Somehow, someone must have talked.

Did someone see us at the library?

Was there someone in the family who was spying on me at campus?

Could anyone have seen me going into Vik's penthouse?

Questions ran in a barrage through my mind, overwhelming me to the degree that I suddenly felt light-headed.

I couldn't understand how my father could know anything about what I'd been up to. My guards weren't ever close. And knowing where the cameras were located at my apartment building, I made sure to leave and get inside without his being in the range of the camera's lens.

"I'm not," I said at last, shaking my head.

"You fucking lying bitch." He clenched his jaw, grinding his teeth as he walked away again, as if the sight of me was too terrible to manage. "You think you can just waltz around and fuck your way through the campus?"

I shook my head. My God, that was so far from the truth it was laughable. I had to force myself to socialize at all. My guys annoyed me and I had to practice not letting my resting bitch face show all the time.

"You just had to sleep around."

"No. I didn't."

"I know you did! I know you've been fucking some moron you met there."

I was tempted to fight back, to put him on the spot and ask how he knew or how he thought he knew anything at all about what I'd been up to. Asking him to clarify what he knew or had heard would just come off as a confirmation that he was right, though.

"I couldn't believe it when I heard. I kept thinking to myself, no, that can't be true. I didn't raise a dumbass. I thought, no, you can't be that fucking stupid."

He doesn't know. Tense and waiting for him to mention Viktor, or that I had slept with one of my professors, I tried to accept that he didn't know. He was mad, but he didn't seem to care about who, precisely, I'd slept with. Just that I had.

"I don't know what you're talking about," I said as calmly but firmly as I could. Feigning innocence and ignorance felt like a tricky attempt at escaping his wrath. It was clear that I had to tone down the heat of this moment. I had to de-escalate this situation. If he merely thought I was fucking up or doing something wrong, he could take out his anger on Maxim.

"You don't know." He growled, laughing maniacally like I'd spouted utter nonsense. "You hear that?" He flung his hand at Peter and the other guard who'd come into the room. "She claims that she doesn't know what I'm talking about. What a fucking joke."

"I don't," I insisted. "You heard wrong." That was a lie. I had slept with someone, only one, and I felt so stupid to want him to be the only man I would ever have in my life. But I would take that secret to my grave.

"I ask you to do one thing. I expected you to be there, not to party and sleep around, but to find out who is trying to take over that area and claim it." He ranted on, repeating the same thing, too stuck in his head and not even open to listening to anything but the sound of his own voice. "I thought I had one child to count on. One fucking kid to rely on. Is it so hard to expect to have one worthwhile offspring? Huh?" He flung his arms out. "You're goddamn useless to me now! Do you realize that? You're damaged goods."

I crossed my arms, refusing to let him see me cowering in fear or shame. Sleeping with Viktor didn't make me worthless.

"You're supposed to remain a virgin, you stupid bitch!"

I narrowed my eyes. "What does it fucking matter?" He was getting hung up on a non-issue. *I* knew I wouldn't be married off. Because I would kill him before that happened. "You never intended for me to marry into the Ilyin family, anyway. You were just humoring them and letting them think I would. So what does it even matter now?"

He seethed, scowling at me. "The option of that illusion is gone now," he growled. "No one else would even be interested in you as a bride because you're damaged goods now. You threw away your virginity for some moron at college."

I shook my head, debating how quickly a guard would shoot me if I attacked him now. Letting my rage fuel me, I imagined wrapping my hands around his neck for ever thinking I wasn't a human or a person or a daughter, but a *thing* to use as a token of business. I could feel the imaginary squeeze of my fingers digging into his pudgy neck, choking the life out of him. Watching the panic fill his eyes would be a victory I would cherish forever.

I could do it.

I would do it. I'd kill him someday soon. As soon as I could secure some money to escape and plot the timeline of running as far as I could with Maxim, I would make it happen.

But I had such limited cash socked away, with him always watching and controlling every penny I spent. I didn't have a route of escape yet, no means to physically get away and not for long. I had to continuously sweep my apartment for bugs and trackers that the guards placed, disabling them every time I found them.

Today wouldn't be the day. Today couldn't be the day. I wasn't prepared yet, and I cursed myself for paying so much time and attention on Viktor and the grand feelings of security and affection that wouldn't save me for the long-term. I had to be focusing on getting out of here, on making sure Maxim could escape with me and not suffer.

I stormed out of there, turning my back on him and not slowing until I reached the car. The driver was out there, but my guards weren't.

"I want to leave," I bit out. That was the honest truth, the whole truth. I wanted to get out of here for good. The racing tempo of my heart wouldn't calm down, and I tried to ignore the prickling sensation of being so anxious. So trapped.

It wasn't anything like when Viktor preyed on me at the library. Or in his bedroom. And I wanted that. I needed him, for no other reason than to stop this panicky feeling of being ungrounded and lost.

Peter and the other guard rushed out, glaring at me for not waiting until I was dismissed.

The driver glanced at them, then sighed and flicked his cigarette to the ground. It seemed waiting for me to come out for a ride was when he always took his smoke breaks. Lately, my patience and willingness to be near my father were getting trimmed shorter and shorter.

"Yeah. Let's go." Peter shot me a dirty look as I got in the backseat.

With my pissy, hulking guards in the front and next to me, I was taken back to school. But that wasn't good enough. The distance from my father helped. He could be mad and rant and pace all he wanted. I didn't have to stand there and take his verbal abuse. The sight of my apartment building didn't comfort me, though. It felt like another trap, another cage.

"I'm going to the library," I said, not caring what the guards thought of that. They didn't follow me, leaving me to my own devices.

On the walk there, fuming and a little scared of what would happen to me now, I tried to understand how anyone could have told my father that I had slept with someone.

The only person who came to mind was that jealous redhead from the admin office. The dean's niece, Jessica Nolan.

How could she get word to my father, though?

It hardly mattered, anyway. The damage was done. Someone had talked somewhere, and the word spread.

My fleeting hopes for a future with Viktor felt further from reality now. As I took a seat on the top floor, where he and I had done the deed, I fought back angry tears and tried to think up a new way out of this dilemma.

25

VIKTOR

I told myself to stay away from Irina's apartment building because it would be the easiest way for someone to notice me there. She'd be under surveillance of some kind, and I didn't need my face showing up on any Petrov footage.

Now, that had to change.

Now, I had to take all the steps that I could to make sure she would be all right.

I parked at her building, worried that Igor Petrov would punish her for losing her virginity. I didn't know anything about the man, only whatever any other Mafia brother did. What I was fully aware of was the fact that she never mentioned him. Never spoke of a parent or family at all, just that they were "influential".

If she was fond of him, even just a little, that would show in her attitude and personality, wouldn't it?

Mindful of the ice on the sidewalk, I jogged toward the entrance of her building. Before I reached those doors, though, I heard the crunch of snow off to the side. I slowed, ready to attack or hide depending on who was coming. That was how tense I was. That was how fully my mind had shut down to brace for ugly confrontations.

I told Irina that I wanted to fight to make us happen, and this very well could be the moment where I would prove that.

Sticking to the wall around the corner, I stayed out of sight as two Petrov guards walked by. "She's a pain in the ass," the shorter man complained.

"Eh, soon, she won't be *our* pain in the ass," the other said.

I narrowed my eyes, furious that they'd talk about her like that.

"How so?" the first asked.

"The Boss will make an example out of her," the second replied, chuckling.

No. No, he will not. I refused to accept that.

Since they were walking away from the building, unhurried and just moving along, I doubted they were leaving Irina in the apartment up there.

But where else could she be?

If those guards sounded annoyed by her, she had to be feeling the heat. Rurik said "everyone" knew that I'd claimed Irina, that I'd been seen out with her. That meant her guards would know, too. With people ganging up on her or giving her a hard time, she'd be threatened and upset.

She'd want to feel safe.

I backed up then broke into a run for my car. I knew exactly where she would be.

The library.

She said she went there late that one night because she wanted to feel safe. I had to hope that would still be true today.

After I drove to the closest parking lot near the huge library, I got out and hurried inside. Just like the last time when I looked for her here, I checked every floor. I shouldn't have been surprised to find her on that top floor again. It was a quiet oasis of glass walls and thousands of books on cases arranged in something like a maze.

Unlike that last time I sought her out here, I didn't slow down and appreciate the slow buildup of tension in stalking her down the aisle. I almost ran, aiming a direct path for her seated at a chair near the windows.

Gray clouds hung fat and low outside, almost as if the sky were pressing down on the roof and walls, ready to snap them all under the pressure.

With her feet under her, she slanted over the armrest and hugged her knees, staring out at the bleak nothingness out the window.

"Irina."

She jumped a little, whipping her head around at my voice. Her expression was tight, a furrowed brow of a deep frown, but as soon as she realized I was there, she crumpled. Almost seeming near tears, she got up and ran to me.

I caught her easily, wrapping my arms around her.

She knows. If she was acting like this, she definitely knew that our secret wasn't such a secret anymore.

"People are gossiping that we..." She burrowed her face against my chest as I held her.

"Yeah," I agreed with a long, rough exhale. "People have been talking about us."

She sniffled, holding on to me tighter. "I'm... This isn't—"

"Shh." I stroked her hair back and let her cling to me, wishing I could whisk her away and envelop her in my security. I could keep her safe. I *would* keep her safe. But I couldn't begin to do that here.

"Come on." I tipped her chin up so she'd face me. "Let me get you out of here. We'll talk."

Nodding jerkily like a bobblehead, she walked with me. I set my arm around her shoulders, tucking her against my side. With a protective stance like this, I wanted to be ready to ward off anyone who tried to bother us. Walking out to my car with her was a clear sign that I was with her, but there wasn't any point in trying to hide our relationship anymore. The cat was out of the bag. The time had come to really talk to her and let her share some answers with me. We'd made a mess out of this by catching feelings for each other, but it was done.

We can't be done. I wouldn't let that thought stay in my head. Her easy acceptance of my guiding her into my car gave me hope. She wasn't lashing out at me and furious, nor was she tucking her head down and crying as she ran away like a defeated coward.

No, she was right here with me. She sat in the passenger seat, silent and serious. I held her hand as I drove. Even though she seemed too upset to talk right now, that would change as soon as we got to my home.

Rehearsing how I would start this conversation filled the ride for me. I knew I would need to be in charge of this discussion, so it was with a twist of gratitude that we didn't speak on the way home.

Once I had her inside, though, I led her to sit on the sofa where I'd spanked her sexy ass and filled her pussy with my cum. It seemed like that had happened so long ago—too long ago—but it was so recent in reality.

"Irina?" I sat on the edge of the coffee table, facing her. Resting my elbows on my knees and leaning forward to clasp my hands together, I stared at her beautiful face. If only I could wipe off the anxiety evident there. Instead, I was here to drop a huge bombshell on her, one she never could've expected.

"I—"

She shook her head and lifted her arm. Pressing her fingertips to my mouth, she gave me the cue to shut up and let her talk first. That wasn't ideal. It wasn't how I imagined this to go, but I could be patient. She looked too worked up to try to argue with her. That was how deeply I worried about her and wanted to keep her as safe and happy as possible.

"Someone..." She stopped, shaking her head. "No, not someone. The only person I can think of to blame is Jessica. She's the only person who could've seen us together."

No, not true. Lots of people saw us walking through that whorehouse together. That was the ground zero of where the word spread from.

"If Jessica didn't run her mouth and gossip about us, then someone else did." She lifted her shoulders and let them fall again, listless even in that motion. "All that matters is that people in my circle were talking, and word got back to my father." She didn't blink or try to hide as she gazed at me. "My father is upset about the news that I hooked up with you, and that's... a very delicate situation to survive."

I nodded, wanting to let her know that I didn't need her to spell it all out for me. But she was on a roll, not stopping as she rambled without pausing for a breath.

"This isn't a typical father-and-daughter clash. I haven't merely disappointed him. I've made him furious, Vik. He's livid about the news that is spreading about me. The news that I'm no longer a marketable or desirable virgin bride any man would want."

I leaned forward to set my hands on her thighs. "You are. *I* want you." *More than I should.*

She placed her hands over mine and lowered her gaze. "When I say my father is angry with me, it's not a simple grudge. I told you that he's influential, but I didn't explain any further. My father is the boss of a Mafia family, Vik. So when he's upset, he can and will retaliate with swift and certain punishments."

"Deep breaths, sweetheart," I urged her as I watched her pant too quickly, as if she were on the verge of a panic attack.

She growled lightly. "Deep breaths won't change that he's so mad, Vik. Nothing can stop him from being furious that I hooked up with a civilian, a normal man like you, when he'd been so sure of my staying a virgin. My whole life, I was raised with the expectation that I wouldn't have sex until my father picked a husband for me. To remain pure and wanted, not used like damaged goods."

Grinding my teeth, I tried to dispel that thought. "You are *not* damaged goods."

"According to him, I am. I'm no longer valuable since I gave *you* my virginity. Since I chose you, a man he'd never meet or be able to judge."

I watched her, mulling over what she'd just revealed.

He doesn't know.

"Does your father know that you slept with me? Specifically?"

She hung her head slightly as she shook it. "No. I don't think so. I think he's just mad that I wanted to do something for myself, of my own choosing, for once. That I'm not a virgin he can arrange in a marriage with a man not of my choice."

Igor doesn't know who I am. I let out a deep breath of relief that *this* secret was intact.

"He's—"

I grabbed her hands, holding them securely as I rubbed my thumbs over her knuckles. "Shh. Let me explain, please."

She furrowed her brow. "You don't have anything to explain or lay out for me."

"I do."

Here goes.

"My name isn't Viktor Remi. I'm only pretending to be a professor at that college. It's a cover that my boss asked me to take so I could get close to you, Irina. So I could befriend you and gain your trust, assuming that you might open up to me and share secrets about what Igor Petrov is up to."

Cautious understanding showed on her face. "Then who…?"

I didn't let go of her hands as I drew in a breath and said," I'm Viktor Baranov, Irina."

She shot to her feet, moving as though she needed to reply on a survivor's mentality. "*Baranov?*" she exclaimed.

I nodded, standing as well, prepared to steer how this discussion should go.

Shock warred with anger on her expressive face. That icy, aloof, stuck-up smirk was gone. Now, with her lips pressed tight in a firm line and her hands fists at her sides, she was fully invested in unleashing her raw rage on me.

I held my hands up, to catch her in case she stumbled on something and pitched to the floor. Backing up slowly, as if I were a feral vermin foaming at the mouth, she shook her head and felt for the furniture to beat a hasty retreat. "A Baranov!" she accused, giving me an extra scornful glare.

Bumping into the end of the sofa, she used that jarred action to step toward the side. Then more to the side.

Until she sprinted for the front door. Furious and stunned, Irina ran off.

I hadn't counted on this to go well, but I hadn't imagined she'd want to flee from me.

"Wait!" I shouted as I dashed away toward her.

She couldn't leave. I wouldn't let her get away, not with the knowledge that I was her enemy. And not with my heart ripping in two as I had to accept that she might hate me for how deeply I'd deceived her.

26

IRINA

A Baranov! Viktor was a member of the family my father considered his biggest rival.

Viktor *Baranov*. Not Remi.

The man I desperately wished for a future with wasn't a normal man. He wasn't a sexy professor who spanked me and made me feel so seen and worthy.

He was a Mafia man, someone indoctrinated into a crime organization, just like me. All this time, I'd been marveling at how different and good it was to have the attention of someone from outside my sphere of drama and danger.

Viktor was supposed to represent the other side of the world, the ordinary side where men simply desired women and cherished them. Not my side, where assholes like my father bartered their daughters for the highest price or reward and played mental warfare over the state of their virginity.

I growled, running as hard as I could as the live beast of fury crawled up through me. I couldn't recall another time in my life when I'd been so livid, so furious and angry. It seemed like every cell of my body was rattling and shaking, vibrating with a campaign for me to explode. To scream.

Viktor was a Baranov!

Speeding around corners of the hallways, I struggled to compute how I could've been so stupid. I'd been so blind and dumb, falling for him and surrendering to this savage desire for him that I couldn't deny.

He was the enemy, and I didn't even know. I hadn't been expecting this—at all—and as I ran from him, ran from the truth he'd revealed to me, I hated how hard this shock hit me. He'd blindsided me with his confession, striking me when I'd been so open and vulnerable to him. I wanted security and comfort from him, but he'd ruined the image of that by telling me that he was my damn enemy.

"Irina!" He chased after me, running without pause. Pursuing me madly, he sprinted to catch up and stop me from escaping.

Of course, he would.

He'd been hunting me all along.

This time, he wouldn't capture me to make me feel good.

After revealing who he was, he would now grab me so I couldn't tell anyone else his secret.

"Irina, wait!"

His footsteps sounded so loudly behind me, but I dug in and ran as fast as I could. The need to survive, the need to flee, pushed me to slam my feet down harder and pump my arms to strengthen my stride.

Floor after floor, I dropped down the stairwell. The thuds of our boots and shoes on the pavement echoed in the concrete chamber. But in my head, my pulse roared deafeningly louder, tuning out the sound of him shouting at me.

Before I could think to shove open another door to get out of the stairwell and run down another floor, he caught me. Grunting hard, he jumped down and cleared several steps to capture me.

His arms latched around me so tightly, there was no chance I'd break free. Kicking and flailing, I tried to wrestle out of his grip, but my efforts didn't work. Not this time. The hard bulges of his biceps pushed against my arms. That lean strength in his forearms flexed as he hugged me tighter.

I had trained in self-defense. I wasn't completely helpless. In his strong embrace, though, I had no hope to slip free.

Breathing hard, he growled and fought to hold me close. Still, I resisted. Squirming and bucking, I gave it my all. Every last reserve of energy I had was spent in a matter of survival.

"Let me go!" I screamed.

No one else was in here. I had no one to count on but myself, and I was tired of it. Not long ago, I yearned to be held by this man. I craved his arms around me and giving me that sense of security I'd never felt before.

With the knowledge that he was my enemy, a Baranov sent to dupe me, I had to shut down those stupid fallacies that I could've ever been safe with him.

"Let me go!" I repeated, my voice lower and hoarse from shouting.

He didn't. Of course, he didn't. Viktor was a man on a mission, ready to take me in.

For several minutes, a torturous length of time that felt like a long blur, he held me tight and didn't relax for a second. All that while, I continued to fight to get free. Eventually, I tired, both from having to fight him and the strain of wrestling to no avail. I sagged against him, surrendering. I could not escape this time, and the daunting thought sliced my soul in half.

No escape. It was all I'd dreamed of doing for so long, running away from my troubles, from the prison of my life and finding a safe future.

Only surrender. It was all I'd done since I was born, giving in to what the men in my life dictated of me.

I caught my breath, focusing only on breathing as he maintained the vise grip of his steely arms around me. The more I gave up, the deeper I succumbed to defeat, he lowered with me. On his haunches, he turned me in his arms until I was cradled against him.

My body ached from fatigue. Stress knocked me down. Knowing I couldn't get away, I fisted his shirt and closed my eyes, unwilling to face him. I couldn't look into his eyes and feel the ironic disappointment that he'd deceived me. The one man I'd chosen to let in, the only guy I'd wanted to give my virginity to.

"It will be okay," he said.

I was so spent, I didn't have the energy to laugh, to mock his stupid claim. But I did get a second wind to lash out at him, venting every drop of anger that coursed through my veins.

"Nothing is okay! You lied to me. You deceived me. Seducing me and trying to get me to lower my guard like that— You *tricked* me."

"I had a cover, Irina, and that—"

"You *lied* to me. You just admitted it. You pretended to be someone you're not all so you could capture the enemy."

"Irina, it's—"

I reared back to face him, glaring and damning him for looking so sincere. "Don't tell me how it is. I'm not stupid. No. I *am* stupid. So fucking cluelessly stupid to have ever fallen for any of your bullshit. Are you happy now? Are you happy that you tricked me and seduced me, just for the sake of getting to your enemy?"

"I'm—"

"You fucking lied to me! And for what? For what!" If he'd given me the clearance, I would've bashed my fists on his chest and pounded out my frustration on him.

"For answers, Irina, because you're just as much of a liar as me."

I went still, glowering at him. "I've never told you anything that could be a lie."

"Exactly. You won't open up."

I huffed. "Don't count on me to now! Not after you've tricked me into wanting you." My God, he must have been cracking up in his head every time I said he was just a "normal" man. "Go on," I goaded. "You've got me now. You fucked the enemy's daughter like it was just another job. What are you waiting for? Deliver me like the useless whore I am so your boss can be happy."

He stood, holding me and pushing me until my back slammed against the wall. "You are not a useless whore."

I rolled my eyes, damning the tears burning behind my lids.

"And you're not the enemy's daughter." He slanted closer to me, narrowing his eyes.

"You don't *know* me, Vik."

He shook his head, somehow calmly in control. "I do. I know more than you think."

He could think that. I was sure he'd gotten a file on me to go undercover and pursue me. That hurt more—that he hadn't come for me because he wanted me, but because it was a job.

"Then you know I will *not* be a traitor and tell you a single fucking thing. Oleg Baranov can rot in hell before I let him use me in this goddamn war between our families."

"You already are a traitor," he snapped. "You are not loyal to Igor. You can't be if you helped Eva escape. You made yourself a traitor the second you wanted Eva and Lev to get away last year."

I swallowed hard. My throat felt so raw and dry. That wasn't what stopped me from speaking, though. He'd arrested me with that reminder. I *had* done a traitorous thing in helping them.

"Your actions define who you are, Irina. Not the fact that you were born into the Petrov family," he insisted firmly, searching my face. "You chose to do a selfless thing for your enemy. That is who you are. You chose to trust me. That is who you are."

I shook my head. He wouldn't break me down. I was too familiar with having to look out for myself, for Maxim, to just blindly go along with what others decided. He'd put me in a terrible position, wedged between being captured and expected to tell all versus appeasing my father so he would spare my brother.

"You are a giving, smart woman, Irina, not a mindless messenger. It doesn't matter that you were born as Igor's daughter, that you bear his name. That doesn't make you who you really are."

"I will always be a Petrov," I argued. *I will always be my father's pawn.* "Nothing more."

"Not anymore." He lowered his gaze. "You could be the mother of a Baranov."

Oh, fuck. With everything else going on, I hadn't stopped to consider that we'd had unprotected sex. "That's why you fucked me? That's why you seduced me? To weaken me and bring me to Oleg for intel? And to knock me up and have this leverage over me?"

He shook me slightly, his hands tight on my upper arms. "No!"

"You took me to bed and lied to me just so you could use me."

"No. I slept with you because I lo—" He stopped short. Taking a deep breath, he seemed to seek a pause for clarity before speaking again. "I care for you, Irina. I know those words can't mean much in the face of my identity. I know you will resist listening to what I am trying to explain right now, but I care for you. When I told you that I would fight for us, for that future with you that seems so out of reach and impossible, I meant it. I mean it. I *will* fight for you."

But it won't be enough. It never will.

"I will fight for *us*."

I shook my head. "There is no *us*."

"There can be."

I had gotten fanciful wishing that he could remove my father's influence and I could stay with him for good. At the time, I saw him as just an average man. A professor who was illegally so sexy as an academic professional. Just one person who couldn't handle the heat of the Petrov organization seeking retaliation on him.

Now, though...

He's a Baranov. He's my father's enemy.

As a member of a rival Mafia family, Viktor was associated with a force that could end my father. If he wanted to prove that he cared about me, if he wanted to stand by this statement that he'd fight for me, for us, then he'd have to show me how.

"Just give me a chance. Come with me, and I will show you that it can be all right. That everything will be okay."

I stared up at him, wishing it could be that simple. But it wasn't. "You expect me to be a traitor to my father, to my family."

He licked his lips and looked off to the side. "I expect you to stay true to yourself. And I know that deep down, you care. You have a good heart, Irina. You proved it when you helped Eva and Lev."

"No. That was just—"

"That was what?" he asked. "How can you call yourself loyal to Igor Petrov and your family if you let them get away? How can you stand firm that you're a Mafia princess and nothing else if you let me in your life?"

"I only helped them because I saw how in love they were. I wanted love to have a chance."

He stepped closer, flush against me. "What about others in love?"

No. Don't do this. I couldn't handle it if he tried to further his deception and tell me that he loved me. I was fighting the realization that I cared for him that much already.

"You lied to me. You tricked me. No love can be founded on that."

He watched me closely, then smiled. Smiled! "Now you're the one lying to me. You can't hide that you want me. That you care—"

"So what if I did? It won't erase the fact I am my father's daughter and…" I sucked in a deep breath, feeling torn in two.

"And what, Irina?" He cupped my face, imploring me with his steady gaze to tell him. "What? What is it that is keeping you loyal to him this time when you weren't loyal to him before?"

I sniffled, afraid to reveal the one and only reason I ever tried to appease my father.

"Why can't you believe in my love for you and know it will trump everything else?"

I huffed. He'd gone and said it. Love. A Baranov loving a Petrov. Enemies uniting in the matters of the heart. It was ludicrous.

"You believe that Oleg will just open his arms and let me in like that, huh? That I turn traitor to my father and spill all his secrets, and that's the key to a happily ever after with you?"

He nodded. "It can happen."

"It won't," I stated.

"Because you don't want it to? You want to lie to my face and tell me that there's nothing between us that's worth fighting for?"

I furrowed my brow. "There is. But my love for you will not be enough to override my love for him."

He went still. Stiff and hard, he studied me. "Him?"

I couldn't speak, too afraid to tell him what drove me to tolerate this life.

"Your father?"

I bit back a sob. "My brother."

He frowned, watching me as I lowered my head. "If I don't do as my father asks, he'll… he'll hurt him. He'll take his anger out and punish my brother." Lifting my gaze to his, I let out a deep breath and took a risk to explain it clearly. "If he learns that I've betrayed him to his enemy, if I tell Oleg Baranov a single thing, he'll kill Maxim."

27

VIKTOR

Maxim?

I watched Irina fight back tears. Her lower lip wobbled as she stared at me, brave to the core to face me with this.

"Who the hell is Maxim?"

For a gut-wrenching moment, I thought she was going to tell me that she was two-timing me, that she had another man in her life. As soon as that worry hit me, I dismissed it. I hadn't been bluffing when I claimed she wanted me. I felt her affection. I saw the truth of what her heart desired when she gazed at me. Those baby blues couldn't hide everything. She was damned good at being aloof and icy for everyone else, but I'd seen the real her. The true woman with grit and fear. She surrendered and submitted to me when I filled her, and I wouldn't forget it.

"My younger brother."

No one ever said anything about a brother.

"Maxim. He's fourteen."

"Why is this the first time I'm hearing about this?" I shook my head, ignoring the stupid idea that she could be lying and trying to trick me. The anguish in her voice when she mentioned him couldn't have been faked.

"Because no one hears about him. My father is ashamed of him and hides him. He's never accepted him and considers him a waste of space. Max is deaf, and because of the challenges during his birth, he's always been weak. He's immunocompromised and deaf, and because of that, my father has always hated him. He's always seen him as less than."

"Fuck." My heart broke for her. If her helping Eva and Lev escape wasn't enough to show me that she was a compassionate person, this did.

I gathered her in my arms, hugging her and holding her close. Unlike when I captured her in this dark stairwell, I embraced her with my arms supportive around her slim body, my hands rubbing comforting strokes up and down her back.

"Irina…"

She sniffled. "He's kept him hidden all his life. He's never been accepted as his son. I have to work to get visitation rights. I have to do as my father says and appease him just to ensure he doesn't kill him or abuse him."

"*Fuck.*"

"My love for my brother is the only thing he has to use as leverage against me. I have to report to him, I have to act as a spy and soldier for him, all to keep Maxim as safe as possible and alive."

"Yet you risked helping Eva and Lev."

She lifted her head to face me. "Because I knew I could fudge the truth around how that happened. The Ilyin soldiers were sloppy, and I knew that I could get away with it. But if you are expecting me to go with you and tell Oleg Baranov all I know, there is *no* way I can lie my way out of that situation."

I nodded, understanding so much more now. Why she was so guarded, why she was always calculating her next best move.

"I have been counting down the days until I could kill my father, Vik. I can't trust that he won't tire of Maxim and kill him first. Or me. I can't trust anyone, and as soon as I can, I will kill Igor and run with Maxim."

"No." I shook my head and took her hand, urging her to come with me. This stairwell wasn't an ideal place for saying such things. "You can run to me, Irina. You can trust *me*."

"I thought I was trusting Professor Viktor Remi all this time."

"It was a cover. *I* am Viktor. Nothing has changed."

She walked slowly with me toward the elevator. "Exactly. Nothing has changed. I am still Igor Petrov's daughter. He will still expect my loyalty to him just so I can make sure Maxim lives."

"No. You can lean on me to help you. I will fight for us, Irina." I would remind her every minute if I had to. I'd caught myself from telling her that I loved her in the heat of the moment. I did. But I wanted to confess that later, when we weren't mixed up in this danger and deception. Right now, I had to get her on board with opening up to me.

"But not Maxim?" she challenged.

"I will," I promised as we rode up to my floor.

"I will believe it when I see it." She crossed her arms.

I tilted my head to the side, peering at her confident glower. "What does that mean?"

"I'll turn traitor. I'll betray my father and tell Oleg Baranov anything and everything he wants to know—*after* you see Maxim brought to me, safe and sound."

"Obviously," I replied as the doors slid open. "If Igor's control over you is tied to Maxim's security, that won't change now."

"You'll see to my brother's safety?" She followed me toward my door.

"Yes."

She huffed. "How? You, alone, will ensure that Maxim isn't killed and is safe?"

"I'm never alone," I told her after I let her inside. Just because we were here and making progress, I kissed her hard. "I will fight to always have *you*."

She blinked up at me, so afraid to hope. I hated that she'd been used and treated like a pawn for so long like this, and for something as sweet as being a protective sister to her brother.

I wasn't wrong about her. She wasn't an icy brat or bitch. Of course, it would be something huge to motivate her. Something inherently good.

"And you can be sure that Oleg Baranov will give you the resources to retrieve Maxim and take him from Igor's reach?" she asked, that dreamy, dazed look after the kiss fading.

She snapped her fingers. "Just like that? The Baranov family will risk war with the Petrovs just for my brother's sake? You ask and shall receive?"

I led her toward the couch, sitting with her for a moment before I planned to call the Boss, Lev, and many more. She was sharp, well aware of how our families opposed each other. "Oleg does not want war," I said, relenting to her truth, "but he does want the upper hand over whatever Igor is trying to do."

"I will not tell him anything until I see Maxim is safe."

She was bargaining on me, testing *me* to advocate for her wishes. While it would've been instinct to be mad that she could be so stubborn not to want to give in to me out of love, it was easy to understand her perspective. She was a fighter, a survivor. Instead of seeing this as an impasse and her not cooperating, I viewed this as a chance to prove she didn't have to fight alone. That she could trust in me, in us. No longer enemies, but together.

"I know." I leaned in to kiss her brow, then sighed. "I know. You are not going to surrender anything until your terms are met." And I had to admire her for being tough like that. For the right reason, she was acting admirably. This wasn't a demonstration of her being sassy or rebellious. This wasn't a last-ditch attempt to fight for Igor. She was protecting her brother, and I had to respect the hell out of that.

"So, let me make a call, and I'll start proving to you that everything *will* be okay."

I felt the burn of her stare as she gazed up at me. Nervous, hopeful, scared, and in awe. So many unspoken things passed between us as I stood, taking my phone with me to call my brothers.

Lev was first. I gave him just enough to work with—that I had Irina with me and she would not reveal anything until we could promise Maxim was safe. He contacted several others, soldiers who could most skillfully rescue Maxim.

Because I needed more information from Irina, I returned to find her hugging a pillow on my couch. With the phone on speaker, we had her provide all the details that she had about Maxim's whereabouts and what he looked like. She freely told us everything. Where he used to live. The nasty area he'd been relocated to. What he looked and sounded like. The details about the guard with him. Everything.

I hated how anxious she was, but she seemed slightly more optimistic when the Baranov soldiers interviewed her for everything they could use to retrieve Maxim.

Back in my room, though, I wrapped up the call with Lev.

"You have to tell the Boss," he said.

"I'm calling him next."

"Hurry," he replied, "because this rescue operation will only happen with his approval, Vik. This is a big risk."

I nodded, rubbing the back of my neck. "I know."

"Asking the Baranov organization to essentially kidnap the only son and heir to the Petrov Family, a son Igor has hidden well, won't go over well."

"We're risking war," I agreed, parroting what Irina said earlier.

"And you're not even making her speak up first. Oleg will expect her to talk first. *Then* he'll help her get her brother."

I cringed. "Maybe not."

"Are you delusional?" he barked.

"Maybe not," I repeated.

"Vik. Are *you* willing to risk war for her?"

"Absolutely."

"You care that much for your target? You're serious about her?"

"I am."

"Fuck. I'll set things in motion and look for this kid."

"Good. Time is running out. Igor is already furious, from the sounds of it, that Irina was with me at all."

"But you don't think he knows you're a Baranov?"

I shook my head even though he couldn't see it. "No. I don't think he does. If he did, we'd know."

"True." He blew out a deep breath. "I'll start men looking for him while you speak with the Boss. Don't fuck this up, Vik. Convince Oleg that this is in our best interests while I get this started."

"Thank you." I could always count on Lev.

I ended the call with him and dialed the number for the Boss, praying he would come through for me, to show Irina that I could fight for her and make our future come true.

28

IRINA

Disbelief.

That was the main thing that stuck with me all day. From the morning, when I learned that Igor knew I was no longer a virgin, into the afternoon when Viktor told me that he was an undercover Baranov spy, and then during the evening, when I tried to accept that Maxim just might be free.

Free.

It sounded like a pipe dream, and because of all the long years that I'd watched him suffer and all those years when Igor manipulated me against him, I needed more evidence to believe it could happen.

So many things had changed so quickly. But when I slowed down to think back through it all and analyze it, I couldn't help my anger when I thought about how Viktor had duped me all along.

I fell asleep, crashing from the adrenaline rush of all the ups and downs since I woke up. Seeing that Viktor was still on the phone, pacing in another room, I made myself scarce and didn't get in his way. Despite my anger at being played, I was grateful for his trying to swoop in and be my hero. Seeing him rush to my safety, and wanting to be Maxim's hero, reiterated that he was a good man. That even though I should only view him through the filter of knowledge that he had to be the bad guy as a rival, he was a good man at heart.

I wanted to truly believe that he was *my* man. My hero. That he loved me so much that I could count on him to come through and save Maxim.

But he didn't say it.

That four-letter word seemed so petty now. What did it matter if he said it out loud when he was acting out the depth of his emotion, risking war to save my brother and steal me from my father?

It was because he'd stopped himself from saying it, he caught himself from uttering an I-love-you, that it held so much meaning. As though he didn't want to put himself out there.

He was already showing me so much more love than my father ever had. His Baranov brothers had listened to all I could share about how to find Maxim. He was allowing me to stay here instead of returning to my apartment.

I had to look at the bright side and hope.

After a long nap, I showered. He was still on the phone, but that didn't alarm me. These things took time. My father had a lot of practice hiding Maxim. Yet, I put my faith and hope in my rivals.

As I peered in the kitchen for something to make to eat, someone knocked on the door.

Viktor covered his phone as he approached me from the bedroom and asked, "Can you get that?"

I raised my brows at his trust. He went right back into the bedroom and closed the door.

I opened the front door to one of the last people I expected to see again. I assumed a Baranov soldier would be there, but it was Eva.

"Oh." I blinked in surprise. "I... I didn't expect to see you here."

She laughed lightly. "I didn't expect to ever see any woman here, much less you."

I narrowed my eyes. "Thanks?"

She smirked, passing me to enter. "Vik asked for food to be delivered, and I thought I'd see to it myself."

"Thanks." I closed and locked the door after her, bewildered by her showing up. Eva and I talked during a lab—once—when we were both at college, but that was the extent of our limited association. As peer Mafia princesses, we'd always known of each other, but we were far from close.

"That's my line to you," she quipped, taking containers of soups and salads out of the bag she'd brought. I helped her, lining things up and wondering what Vik would like first. "Thank you, Irina." Eva looked at me sincerely. "For helping me escape that day."

I nodded.

"That took a lot of guts. Only a brave and intelligent woman would defy the orders of her father like that."

"Thanks."

She gave me a dry look. "Okay. That's three times now. You can't be that much of a ditz if Viktor wants you."

I furrowed my brow, sitting since she did. Following others' lead wasn't my preference, but this was so weird that I was taking it all as it came. "So his type is ditzy women?"

She snorted a laugh. "No. Vik's never had a type, but he can't stand idiots in general." She pointed a carrot stick at me. "So if he's so smitten over you that he's got Lev starting a mission to retrieve Igor Petrov's son, you can't be an idiot."

"I feel like an idiot about him," I admitted, feeling free to do something like girl talk with her.

"Why, because he was undercover and wasn't upfront that he was a Baranov?"

That, and how quickly and thoroughly I'd fallen for him. Love made me vulnerable.

"I've been trying to figure out how that worked, anyway." I frowned at my bowl of soup. "My guards never reacted to his being my professor."

"They wouldn't have." Eva shrugged. "Viktor's always been behind the scenes, managing the whorehouses for the family. He used to be a more active soldier when he was younger, but my uncle thought he had good management skills and put him in supervision in an area where weaker men often got distracted."

I mulled over that for a moment, unsure about how to accept that.

"And this awkward quiet you're giving me now means…?"

I searched for the right words. "Well, I was a virgin when I met him, and I can imagine all that he's seen and done and…"

She smiled. "He supervised those places, Irina, not frequented them. I doubt you have worries there. If a man is willing to risk war for a woman, that's saying something." She resumed eating her lunch. "Viktor was also out of the country for a while, going off on a wild goose chase, so no one around here would've seen him out and about. Viktor just made the most sense to go undercover, and it worked well, since the Petrov and Ilyin guards didn't react to his being on campus."

"Do you miss it?" I asked her. "Going to school?"

She shrugged but ended that with a shake of her head. "No. I did, but Lev and I will get married this summer. And I hope we can start a family as soon as possible."

"Lucky you."

She raised her brows at me, and I regretted how snarky I sounded.

"Maybe you'll beat us there."

"Yeah, right."

She set her fork down. "Do you doubt how serious Viktor is about you?"

"No. But I doubt your uncle will actually approve of any Baranov taking Maxim from my father."

She opened and closed her mouth. "My uncle is a wise, careful, and considerate man."

"For those in his family," I corrected.

"True. And that includes Viktor. If Viktor insists on having you as his woman, then my uncle will need to appreciate that."

"A marriage with an enemy?"

Her responding smile was slow but sure. "I think he might have opened his mind about how to perceive you when you helped me escape. Besides, it can happen. Maria, Oleg's wife, was a former rival's daughter. He only married her to thwart a bigger alliance. And they're hardly together. She officially moved in with a retired soldier months ago." She rolled her eyes. "She and Oleg are legally married but can't stand each other, so they live apart."

I suspected she was being conversational to preoccupy me from the scarier things on my mind. "I'm not going to let you get my hopes up where Max is concerned."

"Don't. It's never smart to get your hopes up too high."

I liked her no-nonsense attitude. But I'd remain guarded until my brother was safe and sound. "And if Viktor and I can ever be together, it won't be as a Petrov marrying into the Baranov Family. I'm a package deal with Maxim."

"Tell me about him. Lev mentioned that he's deaf. One of our housemaids has a granddaughter living there. She's also deaf."

"Maxim has never met another deaf child." I signed it to her. "I read up and taught myself ASL to teach him."

"Impressive," she said and signed. "Laura, the girl at the house, is teaching several of us ASL too."

She loosened me up, talking about Maxim. I shared more about him, detailing our love of books and how he wanted to be an artist *and* an engineer when he grew up.

After I told her more about Maxim, she asked about Kelly, and I hated that I had to admit I didn't have much to tell her. "I tried to engage her in small talk, but she was aloof."

"That sounds like her. She really started to pull away from me when Lev and I got more serious. Rurik still checks on her." She paused. "You know the one I'm talking about, right?"

I nodded. "Rurik is still there, just kind of keeping an eye out on things."

She arched a brow. "Just like you were?"

"Nice try. I'm not telling anyone about what I was supposed to spy on. Not until Maxim is here."

She held her hands up in a truce. "Fair enough."

Fair? I was shocked she'd say that. I was holding out on information until I got my way. That was the basis of negotiations. But from her perspective, I was asking them to give in before I did. It was a savage tactic that I hoped wouldn't backfire.

"I know my uncle will appreciate anything you can tell him."

I slumped forward, resting my chin in my hands. "It's not exactly anything huge. Even I was limited to what I could know. Because I'm just the 'worthless daughter'."

She rolled her eyes, commiserating. "Still, you have insider eyes on what Igor is up to. It will help us."

"I'm sure you can already assume a lot."

"That he's trying to take over. That he's not above using the Ilyins. Or us. Or…" She shrugged.

"I would be proud to help bring him down. I've dreamed of getting out from under my father since I was a child. After Maxim was born and my mother passed away from his childbirth, he started using me. To listen in on conversations. To drop trackers. To implant listening devices and recorders. All kinds of spying, all to have him make good on his promise to 'let' Maxim live."

"What an asshole." Eva scowled. "My father is just a drunk. A fool. Oleg is my uncle, but he's always been more of a father to me than Boris. I'm grateful to have had *one* father in my life."

"Like I said, lucky you."

"Maybe *your* luck is turning around now."

I hoped so. I truly hoped that Viktor could fight for me, for us, and we could all have a better life than before.

29

VIKTOR

Lev reported in to me throughout the night, but nothing he said counted as good news.

"He's not there."

I sat on the edge of my bed and buried my face in my hands. "He's not at the apartment near the docks?"

"No," Lev answered on the video call, furrowing his brow. Tall buildings loomed in his background, but he wasn't hands-on with this ops. Because of his recent capture and injuries, and the rise of his power as Oleg seemed to appoint him as his right-hand man, he had to play it safe and not allow himself to be in as vulnerable of a position in the field right now. He was near the apartment building where Maxim Petrov was supposed to have been moved to according to Irina.

Other soldiers had barged in, ready to fight and retrieve the young teen.

"But it looks as though he was there recently. They found clothes, food wrappers, ashes."

I jerked my face up, alarmed. "Ashes?"

"Cigarettes. From the guard. We're checking surveillance in the area. We're not stopping yet." He frowned. "Did you talk to Oleg?"

"Yes." I cringed. "He's hesitant to remove the boy from wherever he's being held." I had yet to tell Irina. I didn't want to. It would sound as though Oleg wasn't committing to rescuing Maxim. He sounded open to it all, but he'd compromised. His order was to locate Maxim, stand by, and intervene if clear and present danger faced the teenager. But not to remove him until further notice. He was taking this development one step at a time, but that probably wouldn't satisfy Irina. If I were in her shoes, I would feel the same.

Lev nodded. "Correct." He'd received the same information.

"Just please, keep looking." I couldn't handle it if something happened to him. I'd never met the kid, but I already knew how much he meant to the woman I loved.

He agreed that he would.

As soon as I lowered my phone, Rurik checked in via text.

Rurik: *You didn't put in a notice to quit, did you?*

"What the hell?" I whispered.

Viktor: *At the school? No. Not yet.*

That was the least of my worries. I didn't give a shit about my cover. I'd only taken that role to get close to Irina, and now that I had, that cover could just disintegrate now.

Rurik: *Because it seems that people are preparing to go through it.*

Viktor: *People?*

Rurik: *Someone from the dean's office? I couldn't tell. I was following one of the Ilyin dealers and overheard some office staff talking about your office.*

I pounded my fist on my knee. "Dammit." I bet it had something to do with Jessica. That woman didn't know when to stop meddling. If I was in trouble for canceling the class this morning, oh, well. But that seemed too fast.

Maybe it's something else.

Maybe someone on campus knew who I was all along.

Viktor: *I'll check it out.*

I exited my room, finding Irina alone again. Eva had come by and kept her company for a while, and I was mildly curious whether she had gotten any information out of her. I doubted it. Irina seemed ready to stay quiet and keep her secrets to herself until we could bring Maxim to her. That was… a work in progress, but I didn't see any reason to worry her yet. I didn't want to tell her that Oleg was kind of working with us but being cautious. As soon as someone on Lev's team located Maxim, I'd tell her. Then she could swap information with Oleg.

"I need to check something on campus, at my office."

She smirked. "*Your* office?" She stood, coming to stand with me. "Are you even qualified to teach?"

I shrugged. "More or less."

She huffed a weak laugh.

"I don't want to let you out of my sight," I added. "So, let's go and get this over with."

"I don't think you have to hover and worry that I'm going to run now."

I pulled her close before she could walk past me to get her coat. Pushing her against the wall, I shoved my body against hers and kissed her deeply. "The only hovering I intend to do with you is in bed, when I'm on top of you and ready to fuck you hard."

Her breath hitched as she stared at me. I saw that spark of excitement in her eyes again, and I knew she was still there, the sassy woman I had gotten to know and love beneath the stress and fear that had been taking over her all day.

"I don't want you out of my sight in case some Ilyin fucker still thinks that you're marrying into their family." I kissed her again, excited when she lifted her hand to grip the back of my head.

"I don't want you out of my sight because I worry one of your father's soldiers could try to get you away from me."

She kissed me this time, frowning at how quickly I pulled back.

"And I don't want you out of my sight when I get word about your brother, so I can update you immediately."

A soft exhale left her lips. "No word yet?"

I gave in to share what I could. "Lev's team found evidence of his being at that dock apartment you told us about, but he's not there now. We've got men checking the nearby surveillance and scoping the area for them."

She sighed, slumping her shoulders.

"As soon as I get word, we will act."

"Did Oleg confirm it, though? That he'll see to Maxim's safety in exchange for all my secrets?"

Dammit. She had to ask like that. "He will."

She furrowed her brow, but before she could argue anymore, I urged her to get moving and leave with me. "The faster we take care of this, the faster we can resume the other stuff."

On the ride to the campus, she asked me more about what I did know so far. That didn't seem so risky. I filled her in on what I knew, which was limited to the second-hand information that I'd gotten from Lev and Eva, Rurik as well. I added more background, too, like how I wasn't recognized because of my time in the whorehouses for so long.

"That's how word got out and spread," I told her. "Rurik alerted me to 'everyone' knowing you and I had hooked up."

"That's all it is to you? I'm just a hook-up?" she asked.

"You know that's not true. But it was my fault. I took you with me to pick up that package at that place, then when we exited through the lobby—"

"Holding hands and walking through that crowded space," she added for me.

"Yes. Someone in there had to have noticed. A Baranov, Ilyin, or Petrov. Hell, even just someone who's bought something from one of us."

"Drugs?" she asked.

I shrugged. "They have been a common thread with whatever is going on at the school."

"I will explain all that I know, Vik, but Igor's never let me in too much. It's just what he's asked me to watch."

I nodded. "We will appreciate all that you can share." And I wouldn't push her to do so until we'd come through on our end of the bargain. She was taking another huge risk for the Baranov family. She helped save Eva and Lev before. And if she wanted to join us officially, through a relationship with me, she had to be able to put her trust in us that we wouldn't be using her for intel like Igor had been.

We got to the school and I parked close to the building I'd taught at for just a month. Not many students or staff were around in the building. No one was at my office, either.

"I wonder what Rurik was talking about," I muttered, hands on my hips as I scanned the office. Nothing seemed disturbed, and the lock was intact.

"Shh." Irina slanted her head to the side, watching the door closely. The front one was open, and no sounds came from the hallway. Instead, she was tuning in to what sounded like a conversation in the closet.

I watched her press her finger to her lips as she beckoned me to approach the door.

I opened it, proving it was just a closet.

But she shook her head, pointing to the top. Light shone through from the adjacent room.

"You really are good at this snooping business."

She shot me a dirty look. "No, I'm really good at moving past my childhood when my father would shove me in a closet when he got sick of hearing my voice."

That asshole.

She entered, walking further into the closet and moving things around. "It looks like this used to be a hallway."

I nodded. "And it was closed off at one point." Finding a loose piece of particle board stapled at the back, I pried it off soundlessly.

We snuck along the hallway, sticking to the wall, and I wondered who was talking. In a twisted maze, we were lured down another hallway.

"It's probably just a couple of teachers talking," I whispered.

"No. We should listen in."

"Are you ever going to be able to stop the instinct to be his spy?"

She shot me a dirty look. "Yes. I'm not being his spy right now. I'm being an independent agent to understand who the real bad guy is around here."

"Easy. Your father is."

She rolled her eyes. "Yeah, because every time there is a complicated drug trade and turf war, only one person is trying to get ahead."

That's true. Even though a slight worry entered my mind at the thought she could be loyal to Igor before she could ever consider herself loyal to me, I had to respect her tenacity to find the truth.

"It almost sounded like someone said *Ilyin*," I whispered.

"And I think I recognize that voice," she replied, almost mouthing only and not whispering.

I didn't, but the time to ask her about it was gone. We'd come upon the door to another office, likely boarded off as a former hallway route. This room hadn't formed the small entrance into an office closet but the back of a bookcase. Through a slit, we saw the occupants inside.

"I don't care how many more drugs you bring in," a young man said, smiling charmingly despite his sinister tone, "but you have to tone down the women being raped."

Irina picked the pen out of my breast pocket—I was still in my suit with a button up and tie on—then flipped her hand over.

Writing on her hand, she inked out *Marcus James*. She pointed, indicating the man inside.

I shrugged and mouthed *no clue*.

She wrote again. *He's a politician.*

I nodded as they argued about drugs and women being raped. It seemed there was a difference in opinions of what was a tolerable amount to get away with.

"I don't care, man. Like, I'm just doing what I'm told," a younger man said from the opposite side of the room. "Y'all can figure out who gets what cut and shit. I just know what cut I want, and 'til that happens, I'm staying out of all this administrative red tape."

"There's no red tape," Jessica argued. "Don't be a dumbass, Jerome."

Irina looked at me after writing on her hand again. *Who's he?*

I shrugged, unsure. We couldn't get a good view of him either, cut to seeing only from his chest down, not his face. He seemed young, both in his slang and way of speaking, but that was guesswork at best.

"Look, we'll talk about this later." Marcus smiled at Jessica before sliding his hand over her ass and pulling her close for a kiss. "You talk to your people, and I'll talk to mine."

But whose people were whose?

They left together, and Irina and I turned back to go the way we'd come.

"Who—" We'd said it in unison, stopping at the same time.

"I don't know," I answered, regardless of what she would ask. Confused and clueless, I tried to understand what we'd heard.

"This isn't just about Mafia families competing for turf rights around the campus," Irina whispered.

I had a strong hunch it wasn't. Even before Irina would give us an expose on what Igor planned, it was obvious that politics were getting involved.

"Things are never as simple as they seem," she muttered.

We reached my office just as my phone rang. I grabbed it, excited and nervous when I saw the caller ID. "It's Lev."

Irina took my free hand and squeezed it between both of hers. She'd been waiting with bated breath, stuck in suspense for a word on finding her brother. I'd spare her the wait for me to relay what my friend could tell us.

"Lev," I greeted on speaker.

"He was taken. The Ilyins came and took him from the last place we followed him to."

"Fuck!"

Irina squeezed my hand tighter as she stared at my phone.

"They got word that Igor reneged on this arranged marriage of Irina marrying one of theirs—"

"He never actually arranged it. It was all a rumor," she rushed to say, frantic. "There was no agreement. He was just messing with them and playing a game, conning them to think an alliance could form when he never intended to see one through."

Lev huffed. "That's not the way they see it. They're pissed, and they've taken your brother."

30

IRINA

"I wasn't promised to them," I told them. Volleying my gaze from the phone to Viktor, I tried to stop the panic from eating away at me. My stomach was a knotted mess, and I grew lightheaded again as my pulse pounded so fast.

"But they think you were," Lev said again.

"It doesn't matter what they think. It matters what they did," Vik said, taking charge. He hurried me out of the office, looking around as we left. Keeping his arm around my shoulders, he guided me to hustle out of there.

Where I was seemed insignificant. I could freak out here just as well as I could at his apartment again. I wouldn't feel right *anywhere*. My brother had been my responsibility for so long, and my failure to keep him safe would follow me everywhere. It was a stain on my soul, a crack on my heart that couldn't be repaired.

"This is all my fault." I tried to take comfort from Vik's presence. I tried to remind myself that it wasn't just me looking out for Max now. I heard all the Baranov men starting an operation to get him out from under my father's reach.

"If I'd just done what he asked. If I just listened and—"

"No," Vik said firmly. "No. You will not be trapped and be Igor's slave anymore."

"But if—"

"We will find him, Irina," Lev added. "Oleg is aware of the situation and he's not going to abandon you to Igor. Not after you helped to save my life."

I swallowed hard, touched that he could care.

"*I* won't give up on your brother either, Irina. I owe it to you for helping Eva."

I opened and closed my mouth, unable to reply.

"You are *not* alone anymore, sweetheart," Viktor told me once we stepped out into another damn snowy night. I was so sick of this weather, but even my loathing for the snow couldn't stop me from feeling so distraught.

"Go to the house," Lev said. "Take her to be with Eva. Oleg wants to speak to her anyway," Lev said.

Anger solidified in my heart. These men could try to coax me into trusting them, then turn around in the next instant and suggest that I surrender first? They hadn't delivered on getting Max to safety yet, but they expected me to spill all I knew to their Boss?

"I'm not—"

Viktor plowed past whatever I could've said through the anger. "We're heading there now."

He hung up, and I glared up at him. "Vik, I'm not talking before I know Maxim is all right."

"I heard you. Loud and clear. But I think Oleg wants information about him, whether there is another way he can figure out a solution to getting Maxim out of anyone else's control."

I furrowed my brow, disliking how much it seemed like he was placating me. Yet, that sort of made sense. No one knew about Maxim. Not even the Baranov Boss. I didn't understand what other details could help, but I wouldn't be shy to provide anything that would get my brother to safety.

When I arrived at the Baranov headquarters, the mansion that the crime family called a "house", I felt nauseous and weak from the stress of the last twenty-four hours. Viktor was perceptive as ever, holding my hand and offering me support by keeping close. I never had the opportunity to lean on someone. It was always just me. Only me. But the option of having someone else still felt so surreal.

Oleg stood in front of a large fireplace in what looked like a study. The scent of cigars wafted in the air, but it wasn't cloying and gross like all the cigarettes the Petrov men smoked. Eva got out of a chair upon my arrival, frowning with worry.

"We'll get your brother back," she said.

"We will do all we can to try to get her brother back without starting a war," Oleg corrected.

I tore my gaze from her to frown at him. That didn't sound like a refusal to help, but it also didn't sound like a firm vote of confidence that he would get things done, regardless. Keeping my mouth shut, I stared down the rival boss. The one I didn't have to appease like I had with Igor. One I had yet to really meet to form my own independent feelings about him.

He looked fit compared to the wreckage my father had done to his body, but he bore enough similarities that there was no way I'd mistake who he was. He was a boss. A leader. The stern glint of command in his old eyes was unmistakable, but I had yet to fully accept whether he would be *my* boss.

"Nice of you to join us, Irena." His welcome was probably sincere, but I heard the test in his words.

"Nice of you to negotiate with me," I replied.

He almost smiled, but it might have been a sneer, too. "How is it that I never knew Igor had a son?"

"Were you supposed to know?" I asked.

"Was there a reason he had to hide him?" he challenged.

I heaved out a deep sigh. "He's never loved him. Never cared for him."

"It doesn't sound like he's ever cared for you, either," Viktor said.

"Yet he never hid her away," Oleg pointed out. "I want to know why Igor hid his son."

"He saw him as worthless. Useless. An embarrassment because he's deaf and weak."

Another man stood in the background, shaking his head and nearly stumbling in his steps. "No." He slashed his arm through the air, but I couldn't tell if he did it to steady himself from falling in this drunken stupor or if he was adamantly telling us to think otherwise about what we said.

"Boris," Oleg warned. "Not now."

Eva winced, as did Lev.

I could smell the reek of alcohol while Boris Baranov stumbled a yard away. He was drunk, obviously, but determined to insert himself into this conversation.

"Just sit down," Eva said, almost blocking him from reaching Oleg.

"No. No!" Boris flung his other arm out, sending the amber liquid in his glass sloshing over the rim. "He died."

"What?" Oleg scowled at him.

"The boy died." He shook his head, grimacing as he tried to reach his older brother.

"What boy?"

"The boy. He died with her."

I gaped at him. "The boy? My brother?"

Boris squinted, looking at me like he couldn't stomach the sight of me. "You look just like her. You look…"

"Oh, God." I felt all the blood drain from my face. I went numb with realization and dreaded that this old, fumbling drunk could be saying what I suspected he was trying to get out.

My father hated how much I looked like my mother, especially once I lost my girlish looks and matured into a woman.

Oleg sharpened his gaze, looking from me to his brother.

"What am I missing?" he asked.

"The boy died, Oleg." Boris hung his head and rubbed his temple, oblivious that his drink had spilled out. "The boy died with his mother."

"What boy? Maxim?" Oleg faced me.

"He's alive." I shook my head, unable to believe what I was hearing from this drunk. "Maxim is alive. He was deaf and left with several issues from a traumatic birth. A birth my mother didn't survive."

"Oh, shit," Viktor whispered, catching on.

Eva had paled too.

"I was told that he died," Boris said, louder but not clearer. His slurred speech was consistent, but he was determined to speak. "I was told Anna died. She bled out, but the boy didn't make it either."

Oleg glowered at him. "How would you know?" he ordered.

"Because he was my boy." Boris stared at his sibling with sad eyes.

"Oh, God," I repeated.

"You slept with Anna Petrov?" Oleg roared.

Boris flinched, lifting his glass to his lips for a comforting drink, but he realized it was empty. "I... I did. I'm sorry. I didn't mean to, but she was so miserable and we were talking, and... I did. Anna was carrying my son, but she told Igor that it was his."

I covered my mouth, stunned beyond belief. "But he's alive."

"Who told you the boy died?" Oleg said.

"Igor," Boris said. "He told me that Anna passed away and the baby did too."

I shook my head. "Maxim is very much alive."

"That's why he hid him," Eva guessed. "He hid him because he was a bastard."

"Maxim is a son of Baranov blood?" Oleg asked, frowning at his brother.

Boris nodded. "I never wanted to tell you. You would be so furious that I'd complicated family politics."

"Of course you fucking have!" Oleg roared.

Once again, Boris flinched. "I never thought it would be an issue. I never thought anyone would know. She didn't make it and I thought he didn't either."

"Igor must have done a paternity test," Eva said.

Oleg nodded. "And when he saw he had a son of *our* family, he kept him all this time."

Viktor narrowed his eyes. "Probably to use against you when the time is right."

Oleg growled. "Yes. Most likely, that devious fucker."

"I thought…" I staggered to sit. "I thought that he just hated him because he was deaf and weak, not a strong soldier."

"Maybe that too," Oleg said, "but more so, to use him as a pawn. To hold him over the Baranov name."

"Anna was so miserable with him," Boris said. "With how much Amelia nagged me about drinking too much and not being a leader at all, I wanted to feel like a hero to someone. So, I caved. We had an affair and agreed to hide the boy as Igor's."

"Is that why my mother left?" Eva demanded hotly.

Oleg sighed. "Eva, we don't know if Amelia left or if she was taken."

"But if she needed a reason to run away," Eva said, hands on her hips, "that would've been it!"

Boris shrugged, again lifting his glass to his lips, forgetting again that it was empty. "I think it was the last straw. It very well might have been a reason for Amelia to want to leave. To leave me for cheating, to leave this family."

"You fucking imbecile." Oleg turned from his brother to Viktor. "Handle this. Call Lev and update him." The Boss looked at me, eyeing me seriously. "Igor will just have to deal with both of his children being Baranovs now."

I gaped at him as he turned to leave.

That sounded a lot like a rough acceptance, even a coerced introduction, to his family.

I'd only be a Baranov if I married into the family, but I couldn't think about that.

I had to smile at what else he'd said.

Maxim was a Baranov. By blood.

"Bring that boy here," Oleg said over his shoulder, shaking his head as he walked out. "Tonight. Or *I* will wage war against him for taking one of our own."

31

VIKTOR

As shocked as we were at Boris's admission of being Maxim's father, I had to act now. Even if Oleg hadn't ordered me to retrieve Maxim immediately, I would've wanted to do so for Irina. Oleg wouldn't have turned the teen away. He wasn't going to cast Irina out as an enemy anymore, either. I saw how he nodded at her with respect, appreciating her act of goodwill to help Eva and Lev like she had.

"Irina, stay with Eva while I help them."

She nodded, still looking so shell shocked that I wondered if she ever realized what she was agreeing to. Eva wasn't any better. She seemed mad, and shocked, too.

"Let's just…" Eva didn't finish speaking, gesturing for Irina to walk with her. "We can, um…"

"Show her the guest suite," I suggested as I headed toward the door. "Prepare a room for us. And one for Max."

The women stuck together, walking away, but Irina cast one more glance over her shoulder at me.

"I will find him," I promised. "And we will bring him home."

I ran out to my car, already calling Lev.

"Hey, we've got a good location for him, and—"

"Do *not* let anything happen to him," I ordered.

"I know, but—"

"You don't understand. Maxim is the bastard son of Boris and Anna Petrov."

I rendered him silent for a full moment as I sped down the drive.

"Boris… Baranov?" he asked, doubtful and so confused.

"Yes!" I held on for a sharp turn past the gates. "Give me the location. We need to bring him home. Safe. *Now*. Oleg ordered it."

"Holy shit." Lev didn't waste any more time on his shock. He sent me the coordinates of where Maxim was held by Ilyin forces, and I didn't waste any time getting there.

Lev hung back, but he ran up to meet me on the street.

"What the fuck is this?" I asked, gesturing at a whorehouse. It wasn't one of ours, but competition.

Lev shrugged. "It seems like they're trying to hide him there. Or hold him there until they can move him again."

"How the hell did the Ilyins even know about him?"

Rurik ran up from another car, joining us. "They followed Irina's guards. One of them must have switched over to cover for the one posted with Maxim, and they figured he had to be someone of importance."

"So they don't know exactly who Maxim is?" I asked.

Rurik shrugged. "What difference does it make if they do?"

I nodded once. "It doesn't." Because I was getting him out of here and to safety now.

"Who's going with me?" I asked, checking my gun.

Rurik volunteered, and together, we headed to the front door.

"Full fucking circle," I muttered under my breath, unamused that I was at a goddamn brothel after I thought that part of my life was done.

At the door, a woman who used to work at one of the places I supervised grinned widely. "Vik? That you?" She cackled with glee and hurried to hug me. "I ain't allowed to let no Baranovs in here, but for you, mister?" She pinched my cheek as she gave me a side hug. "Go on. Go on."

Rurik grunted a laugh as we stepped inside. "And we didn't even have to pay the cover."

I smirked at him. Finding another whore who liked to move from one place to another, including a couple of Baranov establishments, I asked where the Ilyins were. Rurik slipped several bills in her bra to sweeten the deal.

She winked, leading us to a room in the back.

I opened the door, and before Rurik and I could step inside fully, two Ilyin men stood and fired at us. We were prepared, shooting faster. In the middle of the room, huddled on the floor, was Maxim. He looked like Irina, the same sharp eyes, yet he resembled Eva a bit too. The family resemblance was uncanny.

"Maxim." I spoke looking right at him, so he could read my lips. "Your sister sent me to get you."

He nodded, shakily, and lifted his hand to show that he was handcuffed to the bed.

A whore scowled at us from the side of the room. She wore a bra but nothing else, looking from one dead man to the other. "You're paying for that."

Rurik stepped forward to compensate her while I headed to Maxim. "Got keys?" I asked the whore.

She tossed them over to me, not even taking a break from counting the bills Rurik had given her.

"Let's go," I told Maxim as I helped him to stand.

"Is Irina safe?" he asked. I didn't know sign language, but I understood his speech.

I nodded, making sure to face him so he could read my lips. "Safe and excited to see you."

Slowly, he smiled and exhaled a long breath. Then he reached up to hug me, wrapping his thin arms around me and holding tight.

Rurik stayed back to manage the cleanup of the two dead men. But Lev and I drove Maxim to the house, answering all the questions he asked on the way. Mostly, he wanted to know who we were and if Irina was *really* safe. I was already fond of him, clearly worried about his sister and overprotective in his own way.

Seconds after I parked, the front doors opened. Lev had texted them that we had Maxim and were on our way home.

Eva stepped out, holding her coat close. Then came Irina. She ran down the steps, crying out with joy at the sight of Maxim getting out of the car.

Eva went to Lev, and he held her at his side. Next to them, I leaned back against the car and shoved my hands into my pockets, smiling at the brother and sister reuniting.

"You're so going to get some tonight," Lev joked.

I chuckled. I wasn't in any rush. Irina would be mine. I fought to keep her, and now, we would have the rest of our lives to share with each other.

"I'm going to get married," I corrected.

As soon as I could, Irina would officially be a Baranov. As my wife.

"Oh, going to steal our thunder now?" Eva teased. "We got engaged first."

"I haven't proposed yet. And you guys make it sound like it'll be a long engagement between you two."

Eva shrugged, still watching Irina and Maxim sign and talk to each other excitedly. "I want to wait until Kelly talks to me. I want her to be a bridesmaid, and she's so distant now."

I'm sure Rurik can get a message to her.

Lev chuckled. "It's as good as done, now. You and Irena."

Yes, it is. Thankfully.

"How's it feel to have a brother?" I asked her.

Lev huffed. "Talk about a twist."

"You can say that again. I'm not sure it's fully sunken in yet."

But it would. We all had to adjust to another Baranov in the house. Maxim would receive the full benefits and privileges of our protection—forever.

"Igor is going to be furious when he finds out," Lev said.

"I wonder if he *let* the Ilyins capture Maxim, knowing he's a Baranov," I said.

"To set a war between our family and the Ilyins?" Eva asked.

"Again?" Lev quipped. He'd instigated plenty of drama by killing one of the Ilyin leaders, one that Igor had framed.

"We'll figure it all out," I said. My heart couldn't feel any fuller seeing Irina so happy with Maxim.

We would. Irina would share all that she could with us. She would tell us what Igor had her spying on and why. Whatever trouble Igor was trying to start at the college and around it, we would remain one step ahead.

Deep down, she probably wouldn't feel happy and complete until she killed her father. But maybe I could convince her to wait, to let us bring him down officially now. She and Maxim were safe, and with Igor trying to take a Baranov child and hide him, he'd earned the wrath of the entire family now.

Hugging Maxim again, Irina smiled so brightly, she blinded me. She held on to her brother, hugging him tightly as they took a break from signing and talking, overjoyed to be together again.

As she looked over Maxim's shoulder, she caught my eye and mouthed something I would never tire of knowing.

I love you.

I looked forward to telling her that for the rest of our lives.

"Oh, dammit. I hate this cold!" Eva shivered, ushering us all to go inside. "Why are we standing around in this snow?"

We all hurried inside, and as I approached Irina, she reached out for my hand. She held Maxim's in her other hand, and with a reach up to kiss me, she sighed happily and joined us in the house.

Before she could get too busy catching up with her brother, I leaned toward her ear and whispered, "I love you so much, sweetheart."

She blushed a bit, squeezing my hand.

"Maxim," Eva said, signing to him, "would you like to see your room?"

Maxim gaped at her and signed back, "You know ASL?"

"I'm still learning," she replied.

The teen turned to Irina. "Are we staying here?" His brows shot up high in question.

She looked at me, deferring to me for a moment. "Well, I'm not sure where we'll end up, but we—you—will always have a home with the Baranovs."

His jaw dropped again. "What about Father?"

I shook my head.

"You don't have to worry about him ever again," Irina said. She kissed his brow. "I will have some meetings to get through. I'll be busy with these people, but we will be safe here."

Maxim looked at me, then at the fact that I still held his sister's hand. "Because of him?"

She nodded. "Because of Viktor," she agreed.

The teen smiled and rushed up to hug me. "Thank you, Viktor. Thank you."

32

IRINA

Three days after Viktor brought Maxim to the mansion, I walked out of the shower just as he walked into our room.

"Oh." I raised my brows and smiled. Then I dropped my towel. "There you are."

He laughed, raking his gaze over me slowly. "What do you mean, here I am?" He stalked toward me, reaching for his pants as he approached. "I've been here all week."

"Yes. But I've been talking with Lev and Oleg. Every day."

He nodded, unzipping as he watched me cup my breasts and thumb my nipples. "Yeah."

"And you've been on campus wrapping up your fake job and checking on the activity with Rurik."

"Uh-huh." He pushed his pants down, removing his boxers with them.

"We've been here together but apart," I explained, breathing faster at the heat in his stare.

"For too long," he agreed, stepping out of his pants as he started on his shirt.

We had both been so busy in the aftermath of rescuing Maxim. I came through on my part of telling the Baranov men all that I could. It took days to explain it all. I had pictures and videos too, everything on my phone. I took them back through all the spying I'd done for my father.

It should've felt like I was being a traitor, but I experienced the opposite. I felt brave. Like I was already a contributing member of the *right* family, a found family who happened to fail at being my rival.

Oleg welcomed me, personally thanking me for helping Eva and Lev get out of danger. All the men I spoke with who recorded and noted all that I could share showed me respect, not glares of annoyance like I was a burden or a pain in the ass to deal with.

I also spent a lot of time with Maxim. Eva and I had sat down to explain to him that his father was alive, but we altered that a bit. Boris begged us to not tell Maxim how he was conceived. He had no interest in being a father to a teen, and he felt guilty enough about it all. So, instead, Oleg posed as Maxim's father. He would receive more protection that way, and already, Maxim deferred to the Baranov Boss so well.

They would get along, and I had a hunch that Oleg looked forward to getting to know Maxim.

It was still a big adjustment. Maxim was overwhelmed, and he'd seemed ill at first. The Baranov medical staff helped to check him out, and with ordering clothes and essentials, we invested a lot of time in just settling.

"But that was okay," Viktor murmured as he lost his shirt. He lowered his voice to a deep, sexy rumble of a growly whisper. He fisted his dick and pumped it, teasing me with the sight of what I craved. "Because I know we'll never be apart again."

I smiled, opening my arms to greet him in a hug.

"Never?" I asked, needy for the confirmation that he would be mine.

"You are mine, sweetheart." He picked me up and kissed me. "And I'm never letting you go."

I lay on the bed after he lowered me to the mattress, but he didn't move away. Following me down, he pressed a long, lazy trail of kisses over my sensitive skin.

"Can you be quiet?" he asked with his mouth a breath away from my nipple after he sucked on it, making a bolt of pleasure streak from my breast to my core. "We can't wake up the whole house."

I groaned lightly as he fingered me, making me cream even more, wet and ready for him. "But we won't live *here* forever, will we?" I hated to sound ungrateful, but we'd need our own space. His penthouse would fit all three of us.

"No." He sucked my other nipple, adding another finger into my entrance to stretch me and caress me deep inside. "We'll leave once things are settled."

"Settled?" I laughed once. "I don't think I'm settling for you."

He grinned, leaning up to crawl over me. After we kissed, grinding against each other until I worried he'd drag out this foreplay for too long, I almost begged for him to slide into me. I was young and new at this, overeager to race toward an orgasm. Under him, with his years of experience and expertise, he could show me how to be patient and wait. It felt like a punishment to wait, a disciplinary delay, but every time, he proved to me how the wait could make it all the sweeter and hotter.

"But will you marry me?" he asked, peering down at me.

His long dick nudged at my entrance. I ached for him there. My tits felt heavy and full with arousal running through my veins.

Yet, his question was what stole my breath.

"Marry you?" I asked, suspended in awe and shock that my dreams could be coming true.

"Yes. Will you"—he lined up his wide cockhead to my entrance—"marry me?" He slammed into me in one long, hard thrust. I moaned as he growled, both of us failing to stay quiet.

"Yes." I kept my eyes closed, savoring the burn of the stretch.

"Sweetheart?" He waited to move, keeping his long thickness wedged in me. "Look at me. Open your eyes."

I did, gazing up at him and wincing at the need for him to move.

He lowered his hand to rub at my clit, smiling wickedly and slowly. "Will you marry me?"

I nodded. "Yes," I repeated. Reaching up for him, I urged him to lower so I could kiss him.

He bent, laying his hot lips on mine as he rocked into me. Steadily, smoothly, and without any indication that he'd ever want to stop.

"I'll get you a ring," he said between panted breaths.

"I don't care. I just want you."

"I'll give you a baby."

I kissed him harder, turned on by the thought of starting my own family with him after never having one before.

"I'll give you everything you want, sweetheart, so long as you always surrender your heart to me."

My pussy clenched as the first waves of my orgasm hit me. "You already have it. You already have me."

"Then take me," he growled, coming with me after another couple of deep and fast thrusts. "Because I will never stop loving you."

"Yes." More incoherent sounds and words left my lips as we both reached the pinnacle of pleasure and crashed. The scent of sex hung in the air, and as we slowed down, breathing so hard, our cum mixed on the sheets and glued us together.

After we came down from the high, lying together and nearly dozing off, I looked into his eyes and smiled sleepily. "I love you, Viktor Baranov."

"And I love you, Irina." He pulled me in for a long, tender kiss, squeezing my ass. "I can't wait for you to be a Baranov too."

Me neither.

I didn't have to worry about killing my father anymore. Now that Maxim was safe with his real father and assuming a powerful one, no one could hurt him. There was no need to look back at all the bad times I'd suffered at the hands of my father. All I had to do now was look forward to the future, which would be so bright and full.

I'd found my family at last.

Printed in Great Britain
by Amazon